Spirit in the Rainforest

The Tom and Liz Austen Mysteries

Spirit in the Rainforest

A Tom and Liz Austen Mystery

by

ERIC WILSON

ORCA BOOK PUBLISHERS

*As in his other mysteries, Eric Wilson writes here about
imaginary people in a real landscape.*

Find Eric Wilson at www.ericwilson.com

For information: Orca Book Publishers, PO Box 468,
Custer, WA, USA, 98240-0468.

http://www.orcabook.com

First published by HarperCollins Publishers Ltd.
First US edition by Orca Book Publishers, 2001

National Library of Canada Cataloguing in Publication Data
Wilson, Eric.
  Spirit in the rainforest

  (A Tom and Liz Austen mystery; 7)
  ISBN 1-55143-224-2 (pbk.)

  I. Title. II. Series: Wilson, Eric. Tom and Liz Austen mystery; 7.
PS8595.I583S65 2001 jC813'.54 C2001-910700-5
PZ7.W6935Sp 2001

Library of Congress Catalog Card Number: 2001090781

03 02 01 5 4 3 2 1

Printed and bound in the United States

cover design: *Richard Bingham*
cover and chapter illustrations: *Richard Row*
logo photograph: *Lawrence McLagan*

This book is for
Julia Hardcastle and Verna Hall
Such good researchers, such good friends

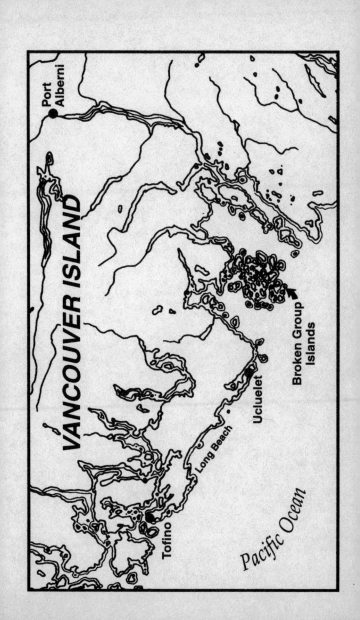

1

They buried Tom Austen just before midnight. For an hour workers had dug while a crowd watched silently. The only sounds were night creatures calling in the nearby forest, and the engines of boats arriving in the cove.

When the workers stopped shovelling, a drum sounded. The rhythm was low and mournful. Then it began to swell, growing louder as more drums joined in.

Gently the workers placed Tom in the hole they had dug.

Dirt was shovelled around him until only his head remained above ground. For a moment he panicked. Then he made himself be calm.

Close by, a native girl was also being buried. "That machine is so big." She looked at the steel blade of a bulldozer on the nearby beach. "Do you think we can really keep that thing out of the forest?"

"This path is the only route the bulldozer can take. Everywhere else the forest is a wall of cedars. The loggers can't move the bulldozer into the forest while we're buried in the middle of the path. And when we're dug out, others will take our place."

"But the loggers don't have to start work in the forest. They can cut down the trees along the beach."

"I don't think so. Look." Tom turned his head toward the giant cedars rising above the cove. Chains were being strung around them, then attached to protesters standing against the trunks. "They can't chop down a tree when someone's chained to it."

"I'm scared," the girl said. "But I want to save this island."

"It'll be saved," Tom said quietly. "Don't worry."

A week earlier, Tom had arrived in British Columbia with no idea he'd be part of this protest against logging the centuries-old rainforest of Nearby Island. He'd simply flown out to be a summer guest of a B.C. family his mother had known for years. But then he'd learned of the protest and had offered to help fight to save the island's forest.

The owner had given a logging company permission to clear-cut every tree on the island.

Environmental groups objected, saying this would mean the destruction of eight-hundred-year-old cedars and the loss of beautiful and important rainforest that was already far too rare. Natives also protested, saying they had never given up their aboriginal title to the island. Plans were swiftly made to prevent the logging by every possible peaceful means.

Now, as midnight approached, hearts beat fast. The contract with the logging company said its workers could come ashore at 12:01 A.M. to begin taking trees, and the protesters waited anxiously to see what would happen. Many of them were natives wearing both traditional costumes and jeans, and ranging in age from round-faced babies in their parents' arms to an old man who wore a braided leather headband and leaned on a wooden cane, his face troubled. Other protesters had come from all over North America, determined to prevent the island's destruction.

"It's midnight!" a voice called, and immediately the drums stopped. At the same moment, figures left the boats in the cove and climbed into small skiffs with outboard motors. Moonlight gleamed on chainsaws in the workers' hands. They would be using the saws, plus the bulldozer and other machines that had been brought to the beach by transport helicopters earlier in the day.

Tom's mouth was dry. The steel blade of the bulldozer loomed above his head, blocking his view of the loggers as their boats began moving to shore. They seemed determined to begin work despite the protesters blocking their path.

A figure left the crowd on the beach and walked toward Tom. She was a slim woman of about twenty-five, with dark hair in braids falling over her fringed buckskin jacket. The older daughter in the family Tom was visiting, Nikki was a member of Greenpeace, a group famous for its struggles to protect the environment. As she knelt beside Tom her brown eyes were serious.

"Are you okay?"

"I guess so, Nikki. I'm a bit scared, but I'm sure those loggers won't do anything crazy with the bulldozer." Tom swallowed. "Will they?"

"If anything awful happens, we'll give your head a state funeral. Everyone will be invited, and we'll try for TV coverage."

"Thanks a lot."

Nikki laughed. "You're part of Greenpeace now, Tom. This is your baptism by fire."

The first of the loggers' boats reached the beach. Two workers jumped out, their faces grim. As more boats landed, the protesters surged toward them. Then a native stepped forward.

"You have entered my people's garden," he said to the loggers. "Why have you brought chainsaws into a garden?"

A man frowned. "We've been given a contract by this island's owner to log it. You'd better step aside."

"Nearby Island is the ancestral home of my people, who lived here for five thousand years before the coming of Europeans. My people have never signed away ownership. We have declared this island a tribal park."

"We've come to log." The man gestured at the workers. "Let's get started."

Immediately the quiet night was split by the motors of the chainsaws. The machines snarled as the workers moved forward. The protesters linked arms and stood before the screaming saws, refusing to move. For a moment it seemed that the chainsaws would just keep coming, but then the loggers stopped. Their leader motioned for the saws to be silenced. Then he spoke into a CB radio.

"Call the police, and tell the owner to get here fast. There's nothing more I can do."

The loggers and protesters faced each other without a word. Once again the birds and animals of the forest called to each other, while moist air blew off the ocean, carrying its salty smell.

"What will happen now?"

"We'll soon find out." Nikki glanced at the night sky. "They sure came fast."

Tom heard a whistling roar, then saw the lights of two approaching helicopters. For a minute they hovered while searchlights in their bellies lit the beach. Then they slowly dropped down.

Police officers climbed down from one helicopter, then watched a door open in the second machine. A man appeared, filling the doorway. He wore large boots, jeans with a shiny belt buckle, and a T-shirt that revealed the huge muscles of his chest and arms. His hair was extremely short, and his eyes looked fierce under bushy eyebrows.

"Wow!" Tom exclaimed. "I expected the island's owner to be pot-bellied and balding and smoking a cigar. This guy looks rough."

"He isn't the owner. He's just the heavy who handles the nasty work. His name's A.X. Edwards, so everyone calls him Axe."

The man picked up a large stick from the beach. Approaching the protesters, he stared into their leader's eyes without speaking. Then, slowly, he raised the stick to the other man's face. Suddenly his muscles bulged and the stick snapped in two. Dropping the pieces at the native's feet, he turned away.

"He gives me the creeps," Tom whispered. Then he watched the helicopter, waiting for the owner to appear. Seconds later he received the shock of his life. Instead of the Godzilla he'd expected, a tiny figure emerged.

"But . . . but, she's a woman!"

"That's right." Nikki sounded annoyed. "Aren't women allowed to own islands?"

"Sure, but, I . . ."

Tom couldn't take his eyes off the woman as she stared at the protesters. Her head was covered with a mass of red curls, and her eyes were pretty even from a distance.

But she looked angry.

For a few minutes the woman and the police officers spoke in low voices. Then she marched swiftly across the beach. "She's coming this way! Maybe you'd better dig us out, Nikki."

"Not a chance."

Reaching Tom, the woman looked at him and the native girl. "You're just kids. Why are you involved in this nonsense?"

The girl spoke up quickly. "My people are protecting this island for me and all the children of the world. This is our park, and one day I will see my own children play here. You can't destroy our trees."

The woman walked quickly to the bulldozer and climbed up to the operator's cab. With a terrifying roar, the engine sprang to life. She switched on the machine's lights, then left the cab and walked to its front, high above Tom and the girl.

"Get out of my way," she shouted above the thunder of the engine, "or accept the consequences. This island will be logged!"

Tom looked at Nikki, who was kneeling at his side with her arms crossed. Now others joined her. An old native woman with white hair knelt beside Nikki, and so did a boy of about six. They were followed by a young man in a leather jacket, then others. Soon the path before the bulldozer was filled.

"I warned you!" the woman yelled.

She returned to the cab and fed more power to the engine. Desperately Tom twisted his head, looking for the police. He spotted them approaching from the beach. But they were moving too slowly.

And then, at that moment, he saw the spike.

It was long and sharply pointed, and it gleamed in the light from the bulldozer. It was held by a man who had just come out of the forest. Thick black hair spilled down from his head, a woolly black beard covered his chest, and his eyes held a strange expression as he stared at the red-headed woman in the bulldozer cab.

Then, as he suddenly ran forward, Tom shouted, "The spike! Stop that man with the spike."

But Tom's warning was lost in the terrible roar of the bulldozer.

2

Reaching the bulldozer, the man shook his fist at the woman and then ran to a nearby tree. Pulling out a large hammer, he began to pound the spike into the trunk.

"That idiot!" Nikki exclaimed. "He'll spoil everything."

The woman was shouting to the police and Axe. They ran in the man's direction, but he dropped the hammer and fled, moving as swiftly as a deer. Within seconds he had disappeared among the trees. The police gave up the chase, but Axe did not. He could be heard crashing through the thick undergrowth, until finally the sound died away into the forest.

Nikki picked up a shovel. "Come on, Tom," she

said wearily, starting to dig him out. "Let's get you out of here."

"But why?"

"Because Mosquito Joe has ruined the protest. Now the police have to clear us off the island."

A large Mountie climbed up on the bulldozer and shut down the engine. "Listen, please," he called. "The moment that spike was driven into the tree, this woman's private property was damaged. You are now required by law to leave her island or face arrest. We will give you thirty minutes."

As Tom watched Nikki shovelling, he sighed happily. "I'm kind of glad it's over. I felt like a sitting duck when that woman fired up the bulldozer."

"She was just bluffing. Vernya's like that."

"She's a local?"

"Yup." Nikki wiped sweat off her face. "Her name's Vernya Anastasia Tosca. Some handle, eh? When her parents died they left this island to Vernya, plus enough money to keep her in fur coats and trips to Europe. But I never dreamed she'd actually log the island. I thought she cared for it too much."

"So why is she logging it?"

"Money, Tom. Vernya's like a fish out of water without a full bank account. This island is massive, and each tree on it is worth a lot of money." Nikki pointed at a cedar which rose high into the night sky. "That beauty may be the oldest living thing in Canada. It probably started growing in the year 1200, if you can believe it. For that reason alone it should be preserved, but it's worth a lot of money logged. Then it could be made into carports and rec-room walls, instead of growing wild and free."

Soon Tom was released. Brushing dirt off his clothes, he grinned at the girl being dug out beside him. On the beach, protesters were being freed from their chains. "Does this mean the logging will go ahead, Nikki?"

"I don't know. The natives are trying to get a court injunction to prevent logging until the question of ownership is settled. The judge will decide soon."

"Who was that man with the spike?"

"Mosquito Joe. He's a hermit who lives somewhere on this island, so of course he's against the logging. Lately some nut has been secretly pounding spikes into trees, and I guess he's the nut."

"Why spikes?"

"Those things are dangerous, Tom. They're twenty-six centimetres long, and their spiral shape means they can't be pulled out of the wood. They also can't be seen once they're buried in the trunk. They don't harm the tree, but if a saw hits a spike its chain could break and injure the logger. So if the loggers suspect the trees have been spiked, they won't cut them down."

"Sounds like a good strategy to me."

"Well, you're wrong. Spiking trees is criminal. Loggers could be badly hurt, and the battle isn't against them. Our fight is with Vernya, and the other big-shots in the city who sit behind fancy desks, deciding to destroy our forests. We're going to stop them, but by peaceful means."

"Why did Axe chase the hermit into the forest?"

"He's tried for a long time to catch Mosquito Joe. Vernya doesn't want him on the island. Listen, I'm going down to the beach to help take the chains off the others. Then we'll get in my boat and head home."

As Nikki walked away, Tom looked around at the trees towering above him, black against the moonlight.

Suddenly he heard a faint call from the forest. It sounded like a human voice. Tom glanced over his shoulder. Nikki was down on the beach. Most of the other protesters were already heading toward their boats, while Vernya, the police and a few loggers were clustered around the helicopters.

Tom walked slowly toward the black outline of the trees and then moved into the forest. Someone had called. He was sure of it.

From somewhere in the darkness came the trickle of hidden water. Something whooshed past Tom, then the air was still again. As his eyes slowly adjusted to the darkness, he moved forward and entered a small clearing. Above him were the cold, clear stars.

A terrible *screech!* sounded in the night. Was it the hermit calling for help? Then the sound was followed by a laughing sob that made Tom's scalp creep. More sounds followed, and he realized he was listening to the cries of many night creatures of the forest.

Kneeling on a boulder, Tom drank from a stream and wiped his mouth. "I'd better turn back," he muttered to himself, then looked around at the forest.

From which direction had he come?

Tom stared at the black trees, suddenly afraid. Trying not to panic, he looked at the stream and realized he could follow it to the ocean. Then maybe he'd see the protesters' boats heading home and could call for help.

Taking a deep breath, Tom began to push through thick undergrowth. Branches scratched his face, hanging moss brushed his skin, and his legs felt like they were wading through deep water as he fought his way past thick shrubs, often tripping over exposed roots and dead branches.

Occasionally he stopped to wipe sweat away from his eyes and listen for sounds. At last the forest seemed to grow thinner. With a final burst of energy Tom fought his way out of the trees and saw a tennis court straight ahead.

A tennis court?

Tom frowned, thinking that his eyes weren't focusing properly. But there it was under the moonlight—a tennis court overgrown with weeds, its nets sagging between rusty poles. In the distance he could see the outline of several buildings.

Tom walked toward them, watching for signs of life. Nothing moved except the tall grass, which stirred gently under a breeze. Although some windows reflected the moonlight, others were hidden under plywood. Rusty stains marked the walls, and a crooked flagpole rose above one building.

Then he heard the terrible sound of a girl's voice.

"Beware!" it cried. *"Beware, beware!"*

3

The voice seemed to be coming from under water. Over and over it cried, *beware!* while Tom stood, frozen with horror. Then he ran. Desperately he raced toward the shelter of the forest as the girl's voice pursued him.

As he stumbled into the shelter of the trees, a shape appeared in the darkness. Mosquito Joe. The hermit raised his arms, making a sound like the angry growling of a dog, and then vanished among the trees.

Turning in the opposite direction, Tom crashed through the undergrowth, throwing himself past bushes and trees that clutched and scratched. Finally he tripped and fell to the ground. As he lay gasping for air, Nikki called his name. "Tom! Tom Austen! Where are you?"

"Over here, Nikki!" He stood up, wiping sweat from his face. "How did you find me?"

"It wasn't easy." Nikki came out of the darkness, shaking her head. "Why did you take off into the forest? There are people everywhere searching for you."

"I thought I heard someone calling. Then something terrible . . ."

"That was a stupid thing to do," Nikki interrupted angrily. "You've got no business nosing around in here."

"I'm sorry." Tom sighed, then fell silent as he began to follow Nikki through the trees. He wanted to ask her about the buildings and the voice he'd heard, but was afraid to. Then Nikki abruptly turned and put an arm around his shoulders. "I'm sorry, Tom. This protest has me on edge. I can't stand the thought of this beautiful rainforest being destroyed." She looked around. "You know, there are more organisms living in a single rotting log than there are people on earth. At this minute we're surrounded by an incredible variety of life. Salamanders, shrews, snails, spiders . . ."

"No wonder you don't want to see the island destroyed. But, Nikki, this girl's voice . . ."

"It wouldn't be so bad if they logged some of the forest and left the rest standing. But the so-called modern method is clear-cut logging, where they take out everything they can and burn what's left. If this forest had been clear-cut, we'd be walking through a landscape almost as barren as the moon."

"That sounds awful."

"We'll stop them, Tom, because we have to. Our generation has to save these forests, or there'll be nothing left. A century from now people won't know what a rainforest was." She pointed to a nearby tree. "It would take twenty people, hands linked, to make a circle around that one cedar."

They started walking again. Nothing was said until they heard a whooshing sound. "I heard that earlier." Tom looked at Nikki. "What is it?"

"That was the Lord of the Night passing by."

"The what?"

"That's what people call the owl. We just heard a screech fly by, or maybe a great horned owl. Their call sounds like a crying baby."

Stars appeared above as they entered a small clearing beside a stream. "Salmon spawn here," Nikki said, "but they couldn't if the island was destroyed. This stream would be blocked by dead trees and land slides."

Tom knelt to drink the cold water. "How big is the island?"

"It's enormous. There's even a small mountain in the middle of it. People think Mosquito Joe lives somewhere on the mountain, but no one knows for sure."

"Has he lived on this island all his life?"

Nikki shook her head. "He came here after the . . . accident . . . at the school."

"What accident? What school?"

"You saw those old buildings, and the tennis court?"

"That's right! And I heard this weird voice. I thought maybe . . ."

Nikki raised her hand as they broke through the edge of the forest onto the beach. "Don't think so much, Tom. It will only get you into trouble."

"What do you mean?"

"That school has been nothing but a headache for everyone in Ukee. Stay away from it, Tom." And with that she sprinted ahead of him in the direction of her boat.

Puzzled, Tom hurried after her. He wouldn't ask any more questions, but he made a silent vow to learn more about the secret of the island.

Even if he had to return to the deserted school.

* * *

The next morning Tom was awakened by a mournful sound. *UGG-Uhh UGG-Uhh*. For a minute he couldn't think where he was. Then he opened his gummy eyes and recognized the guest room in the basement of Nikki's house. From upstairs came the sizzle of bacon, and he knew that Nikki's mother was preparing another of her gigantic breakfasts.

His stomach rumbling in anticipation, Tom crawled out of bed and went to the window. Heavy fog pressed down among the trees that surrounded the neighbourhood in Ucluelet where Nikki's family lived. Again Tom heard the *UGG-Uhh UGG-Uhh* and realized a foghorn was sounding somewhere on the nearby coast.

Upstairs, Tom exchanged cheerful hellos with Mr. and Mrs. Vangelis, then smiled shyly at their younger daughter, Bunni, who was sitting at the kitchen table.

"Where's your sister?"

She laughed. "Nikki's still out like a light. That protest last night really decked her. What happened, anyway?"

Mr. Vangelis tossed a newspaper onto the table. "It's all in here."

Bunni's blue eyes smiled at Tom, and something turned over inside his chest. "Why don't you tell me about it instead, Tom?"

"Sure," he said, trying not to stare at her blond hair, which fell in soft waves to her shoulders. "But let me eat first." Going to the stove, he leaned close to the sizzling frying pan and breathed deeply. "Ahhhhh, that's wonderful. Breakfast is my favourite meal." He glanced at Mrs. Vangelis. "Would you like to know the secret of keeping bacon from curling in the pan?"

"I certainly would!"

"Well, it's very simple. Just don't let those naughty little bacons take their brooms into the pan."

As Mr. and Mrs. Vangelis laughed, Bunni shook her head. "I don't get it."

"I'll explain later, but first I need all my concentration for your mother's fabulous cooking."

Tom put away a heaping plateful of bacon and eggs and toast. Then he left the house with Bunni to look around the town, located on the west coast of Vancouver Island. The moist fog surrounded them as they walked along a street of modern houses. Close by, a hill sloped down to a narrow arm of the sea. Moored at Ucluelet's docks were the gillnetters and seiners that made the town a valuable salmon-fishing port.

"Are you involved in Greenpeace, too, Bunni?"

"Nope. I leave that to Nikki. She's involved enough for both of us." They reached the town's main street, which was lined with large motels. The cars in their lots displayed licence plates from many different provinces and states. "Sometimes I think she's too dedicated. She's been involved in some totally stupid stunts."

"Such as?"

"A bunch of Greenpeace people went into the north Pacific to find whaling boats from Russia. When they found one, they circled it in little rubber Zodiacs until it was forced to stop. Then my sister and two guys climbed on board and hung a sign from its funnel, protesting Russian whaling." Bunni shook her head. "They could have been hurt, or taken prisoner."

"Why'd they do it?"

"Some media people were with them, and their stunt was shown on TV all over the world. But so what? The Russians won't stop killing whales just because Greenpeace hung a banner on their boat."

"But that kind of pressure has made other countries stop whaling. Besides, isn't it important to fight for your beliefs even if you don't win?"

"Maybe," Bunni said, shrugging. "But you can only go so far."

For a moment Tom was silent, thinking about Nikki. "Nikki doesn't like Vernya, does she?" he asked Bunni suddenly.

"She hates Vernya."

"But why? Is it just because of the logging?"

Bunni shook her head. "Nobody in our family will talk about it, so there's no use asking questions."

Tom looked at Bunni, feeling puzzled. *Yet another secret.* "How about the deserted school? What can you tell me about it?" Bunni didn't reply, but Tom kept trying. "I heard the creepiest voice there last night. It was like a girl, calling from under water."

Bunni nodded. "Yeah, that makes sense."

"What do you mean?"

"Other people have heard the voice, too. That's why nobody will go near the school, including me."

"Are you sure? I thought I'd go back to investigate. Why don't you come along?"

"Forget it."

"What happened at the school, Bunni? Did Vernya own it, too? Why the watery voice?"

But Bunni shook her head, refusing to answer. They paused to look in the window of an art gallery that featured sea scenes by local artists, then walked on past a tiny church with moss growing on its white cross. Bunni led Tom into a store that sold books and local crafts. Mounted in the cozy interior was an enormous sea lion. "The tourists all love that," Bunni said, laughing.

When they left the bookstore, Tom pointed at a banner reading UKEE DAYS. "I know this town's called Ukee for short, but what does that sign mean?"

"Ukee Days is the big summer blow-out. There are native dancers and logger sports and a herring-skiff race, and a dance at night." Her blue eyes looked at Tom. "I bet you'd be a good dancer."

Tom blushed, then wished for the millionth time he hadn't been born a redhead. You couldn't hide your feelings when your face revealed every secret.

A black Lab ran to Bunni, wagging its tail. As she bent to rub the dog's ears, a man approached. He had white hair, bristly stubble on his face, and blue eyes that looked suspiciously at Tom. "Another tourist," he said, shaking his head. Then he turned to Bunni.

"Was your sister over at the island last night?"

"That's right, Mac. So was this guy. His name is Tom Austen."

Tom put out his hand and received a handshake that made him wince. Mac certainly was strong for his age. "Do you live in Ukee, sir?"

Ignoring Tom, the man turned to Bunni. "Was that woman on the island?"

"You mean Vernya? I guess so, but I wasn't there."

"I was," Tom said. "Vernya almost took off my head with a bulldozer."

Mac studied his face. "You look young for a protester. Why'd you do it?"

"Mostly for the adventure, I guess, at first. But afterwards I walked through the rainforest and realized how beautiful it is. It shouldn't be destroyed just so Vernya can make some money."

"You're right about that." Again the man gripped Tom's hand, but this time he smiled. "I appreciate your efforts against that woman. She's a nasty parcel of goods."

"Why do you say that?"

"She took away my job. I was caretaker at her school on the island, and then she fired me without warning. It wasn't fair, when I was the only one who stood by her after the accident."

"What accident, sir?"

The man stared at Tom, then turned to Bunni. "Tell your sister hello for me."

"Okay, Mac."

As the man started walking away with the dog, Tom ran after him. "Could I come and visit you, Mac?"

"Why?"

"Um . . . when I get back home I'm planning to write about my holiday here. You know, for school and stuff. I bet you know lots about Ukee's history."

Mac smiled. "Most kids today aren't interested in old folks like me. Sure, come by later. Anyone can tell you where my place is."

"Great!"

Tom watched Mac go, wondering what the man could tell him about the secrets of the school and the watery voice. Then he ran to join Bunni.

Moments later they reached the crest of a hill. At a distant dock was an elegant white ship. "That's the *Canadian Princess*," Bunni said. "It used to be a survey ship, and now it's a floating hotel. It has a fleet of cruisers that take tourists fishing and whale-watching. All spring and summer grey whales feed in the ocean near here. The cruisers take people close enough to see them rolling and plunging through the waves."

"I've heard how great the whale-watching is around here. I'm dying to see them! I've got whale pictures all over my room at home."

"Maybe Nikki can arrange something. In the meantime, let's go look at those boats."

The fibreglass cruisers were moored next to the *Canadian Princess*. As they walked along a swaying wooden dock, studying their sleek lines, Tom breathed deeply, filling his lungs with salty sea air. Over the water, two gulls squabbled over some food. The winner rose swiftly into the fog and was lost in its grey mists while the second gull flew to the highest mast of the *Canadian Princess* and settled there to study the passing scene.

"You're lucky to live by the ocean. But the prairie is beautiful, too. There's nothing as pretty as the wheat rippling under the wind." Tom grinned. "Hey, I'm starting to get homesick."

"Let's go inside the *Princess*. Can you imagine staying in a floating hotel? What a great holiday."

Just as they went on board, a horn sounded from the nearby parking lot. The door of a van opened and they saw Nikki get out, waving. She came to join them, looking sleepy. "I'm here for some breakfast. You two want to join me?"

"Sure," Bunni said, "but I won't eat. I'm on a diet."

Tom smiled. "I could probably manage something. All this sea air gives me an appetite. Thanks, Nikki."

Inside the floating hotel were pictures of guests holding fat spring salmon. "They call those fish *smileys*," Bunni said, "because the people who catch them can't stop smiling." As they walked through the ship, Tom stared at the brass fixtures and polished mahogany. Going below to the restaurant, they studied the menu.

"Smoked salmon!" Tom exclaimed. "Even the words make my mouth water."

"Then that's what you'll have." Nikki looked around for a waiter. Then her eyes narrowed. "I think I just lost my appetite. Look who just came in."

Standing at the foot of the stairs was Vernya Anastasia Tosca. She was wearing an outfit of shimmering silk in an azure shade. The dress emphasized the deep blue of her eyes while perfectly complementing the red curls that framed her face. Diamonds winked and blinked at her ears and throat.

"Looks like she's jetted to Paris again to shop," Nikki muttered. "I wonder how many cedars will die just to keep Vernya in silk and mink."

"Not to mention gas for her Lotus," Bunni said. "Have you seen it, Tom? It's a fabulous car."

Nikki gave her a dirty look. "Must you sound so impressed?"

Tom watched a waiter rush toward Vernya, making loud cries of welcome. "She must be a regular here." As the man led her across the restaurant, Nikki's face fell. "He's going to seat Vernya right beside us. I can't believe it."

As soon as Vernya was settled, she turned to Nikki. "Nikki, dear, how are you? I haven't seen you for ages."

"Your memory must be slipping with age, Vernya. I was kneeling in front of your bulldozer last night."

"Oh, yes. I'd almost forgotten." Her blue eyes studied Tom. "Haven't I seen your head somewhere before?"

He started to laugh, then caught Nikki's look. Smothering the laugh, he said, "You're right. I was one of the kids who was buried."

"Well, I'm glad all that nonsense is over and the loggers have started work. I found the protest quite boring."

Food was brought to their table. Then Nikki turned to Vernya. "Have you really told the logging company they can clear-cut the whole island?"

"There's plenty of other forest left in Canada," Vernya said.

"Not at the rate it's being cut."

"Then the government should grow more trees."

"Vernya, you know that that's not possible. After

all the trees have come down with clear-cut logging, the final step is slash burning. Toxic chemicals are poured everywhere and the land is burned to a crisp. Then the rain turns whatever soil remains into mud where nothing can grow."

Vernya looked closely at Nikki. Then she shook her head. "I . . . I don't believe you."

"Open your eyes, Vernya! Drive along any highway in British Columbia and you'll see the mess from clear-cut logging!"

"My island won't look like that."

Nikki snorted. "Quit fooling yourself, Vernya. Your island is doomed unless you change your mind. Don't let them log it!"

"I'm not sure that . . ."

"Turn the island into a park. People would come from everywhere to enjoy it. There'd be jobs in tourism that would last forever, instead of the few months of work the loggers will get."

"But I need the money now," Vernya said in a low, tense voice.

"Then sell the Lotus, or a couple of your fur coats. If you love this planet, you should save the beauty for everyone to share. Please, Vernya!"

"Well, I . . ."

As Vernya paused, her eyes went to the nearby stairs. She gasped and stood up, clutching her napkin. "Major . . . ! What . . . ?" At the same time, Nikki also looked toward the stairs. Her face turned white as she stared at the man who stood smiling in their direction.

"Oh, no," Bunni muttered.

He was extremely handsome, with wavy black hair

and large dark eyes. At his neck was a silk tie that went beautifully with his blue blazer and grey slacks. As he came toward the table he moved with the ease of an athlete. People elsewhere in the restaurant stared at him in admiration.

Vernya was also staring. "What are you doing here?"

Smiling, the man kissed her. "A bit shocked are you?" His voice was deep and rich. "You know I love surprises, my darling." Again he kissed Vernya and then turned to Nikki. "How are you?"

Instead of answering, she blushed and looked down at the table. As Bunni reached over to squeeze Nikki's hand, the man turned to Tom. "I'm Major Warwick Tosca." His handshake was firm, and his smile friendly. "I'm Vernya's husband."

As Vernya smiled, Nikki stared at her plate. Again Bunni squeezed her hand, then looked at Major Tosca. "I haven't seen you around Ukee for ages," she said brightly.

"I've been away on business. I hated to leave Vernya alone, but there was no choice. Happily we'll soon be coming into real money, so there'll be no more separations." Again he kissed his wife, then sat down. "I've had a long drive this morning, and I'm desperately hungry. What do you recommend?"

Tom smiled at him. "I ordered smoked salmon. It should be excellent in a salmon-fishing capital like Ukee."

Major Tosca laughed. "Then smoked salmon it shall be, followed by the largest steak in captivity." After giving his order, he looked around the restaurant.

"This place is certainly busy. Looks like they've benefitted from my shutting down The Major's Galley." He smiled at Tom. "My restaurant served the best seafood on Vancouver Island."

"I'm sorry I missed it. Why did you close?"

Major Tosca shrugged. "Problems with the staff, problems with suppliers. That sort of thing."

Bunni looked at him. "People say your restaurant was far too big for a town like Ukee. There weren't enough customers to fill it."

"Well, times are tough. Perhaps most people can't afford to dine out." The diamond on the ring finger of the Major's left hand flashed in the sunlight as he raised a gold lighter to the cigarette in his lips. "So, Tom Austen, why have you come to Ukee?"

"My mom is a friend of the Vangelis family. I expected to just relax out here, but then I got involved in the protest."

Vernya laughed. "You sure did get involved, right up to your neck. I have to admit, Tom, you've got a lot of spirit."

He smiled. "Thanks."

"But of course the protest was a waste of time." Vernya looked at her husband. "The loggers have begun work."

"Excellent."

At long last, Nikki spoke. "It's not excellent. The entire island will be destroyed."

"Don't worry," Vernya told her. "The Major has arranged to have the island replanted with young trees using the Finnish method."

"Which is?"

"In Finland, logging companies have to give the government a large deposit of money. After they've got a new forest of young trees growing properly, the companies get their money back."

"You'll do the same thing on Nearby Island?"

"Of course." Major Tosca smiled at her. "Trust me, Nikki."

"I've heard those words before. They didn't mean a thing."

For a moment they stared at each other. Then Major Tosca smiled easily. "We all change, we all mature." He turned to Tom. "I'm sure you're enjoying your visit with the Vangelis family. They're marvellous people."

"I sure am." Tom looked sideways at Nikki. "And, um . . . speaking about the island, there are a couple of things I was wondering about . . ."

Nikki shook her head. "Leave things alone, Tom. I've already warned you."

Major Tosca looked at Tom. "What are you curious about?"

"That deserted school on the island. I got the scare of my life last night. I heard this creepy voice crying *beware*. Then, as I ran away, I was almost attacked by the hermit."

"Oh, yes, Mosquito Joe. Axe was supposed to clear him off the island, but he failed."

"I'm not surprised. The guy moves as silently as a shadow."

"I agree with Nikki, Tom," Major Tosca said seriously. "Leave things alone. Don't go near the school."

"But I'm thinking about going back."

Vernya shook her head. "That school is my property, so keep away." When Tom smiled, her blue eyes narrowed. "Don't try to charm me with that smile, young man. Stay away from my school."

"But. . ."

"I'd listen to my wife, Tom," Major Tosca said. "She's tougher than she looks. Don't let this pretty face fool you." Again he gave his wife a kiss, then hugged her as she leaned against his shoulder. "Love is strange, and love is wonderful."

Nikki threw her napkin on the table. "Any more of this gooey love stuff and I'll toss my cookies." Standing up, she looked at Major Tosca. "I'm glad you'll be protecting the island. Your wife never would." Before Vernya could reply, Nikki turned to Bunni and Tom. "Let's get going."

Nothing more was said until they emerged on the deck of the *Canadian Princess*, and Bunni put an arm around her sister. "You shouldn't get so upset with Vernya."

Nikki's lips parted in a forced smile. "That worm of a woman doesn't bother me." Her eyes flashed toward the portholes along the hull of the ship. "Vernya is probably sitting behind one of those portholes right now, cuddled up to her husband and watching us with a smirk on her pretty-pretty face. I'll bet she's waiting for us to drool over her car."

"The Lotus?" Bunni exclaimed. "Where is it?"

"Parked behind that tour bus, but *do not* go and see it. I don't want to give Vernya the satisfaction."

"Okay." Bunni rolled her eyes dramatically, then shook her head. "But it's really too bad. The Lotus is candy-apple red, Tom. You'd love it."

"Don't tempt him." Nikki walked to her van and got inside. "Stay away from the car."

"Sure thing, Nikki. You can trust us."

But the moment the van had disappeared over the crest of the hill, Bunni grinned at Tom. "Come on! Let's have a quick look. Nikki will never know."

Tom hesitated. Then he looked across the parking lot. "You know, I've never seen a Lotus in real life."

"Then come on!"

They raced across the lot to the car, which was as fabulous as Tom had hoped. For a long time he walked around it, studying the body as it glistened under the sun, and staring in the windows. Then, just as he had finished memorizing every detail, he heard the crunch of wheels on gravel and turned to see the van approaching across the parking lot.

Nikki slowed down, gave Tom and Bunni a dirty look, then drove angrily away.

4

An hour later Tom arrived at Mac's house. He was still feeling guilty about the Lotus, but he couldn't understand why Nikki had been so angry. Why did she hate Vernya so much? Nikki didn't seem like the kind of person to be jealous of Vernya's money. She was concerned about more important things than that. Tom couldn't figure it out.

Mac's place was an old wooden house which was so close to the harbour that it actually stood on stilts above the water. A small creaking bridge connected the house to the shore. As Tom crossed the bridge he almost felt like looking down for trolls. Then he knocked on the door.

"I've been looking forward to your visit," Mac said, inviting him inside. "I've got some things to show you."

The black Lab came over to Tom, tail wagging happily.

"I really miss my cat," Tom sighed, rubbing the dog's neck. "He's back home in Winnipeg."

"I grew up there. Worked in the railway yards. Then I lost my best friend in an accident. There were too many memories for me to stick around. So I moved to B.C., and I've stayed put ever since."

Tom looked around the small house. He'd expected it to be jammed with musty furniture and photographs turning yellow in their frames, so he was surprised to find it neat and bright. Beside an easy chair was a table piled high with books and magazines, and there was a small desk and a wood stove. Mac also had a ghetto blaster with many CDs, and a mattress on the floor under tall windows overlooking the ocean.

"Wow, Mac, are you ever lucky to sleep on the floor. I've begged my parents to throw away my bed so I can do the same, but they won't let me."

"When you're an old fellow like me, nobody sets any rules." Mac rubbed the Lab's head. "Except for Hogan, of course. He's the boss around here. I never go anywhere without him."

Tom went over to the ghetto blaster. "Hey, you've got some of my favourite music here!"

"You sound surprised."

"Well, I, um . . ." Tom looked down at the CDs, shielding his blushing face. "I thought, uh . . ."

"You thought I'd have mouldy old music? Bing Crosby, and people like that?"

"I guess so."

"Well, I'm glad I fooled you." Mac picked up some CDs. "I like music, and these youngsters are pretty good. Their clothes are strange, but they know how to sing. Don't get me wrong. I also enjoy oldtimers like Mozart and Beethoven. Those fellows in their wigs sure understood music." After putting on a CD, he led Tom to a door. "Let's talk out here."

A large wooden deck extended over the ocean. The view was spectacular. Tom leaned against a rail, studying the many fishboats anchored at Ukee's docks. "That's mine," Mac said, pointing at an orange motorboat rocking in the waves beside a nearby dock. "You should come fishing with me some time."

"Sounds great." Tom sat down in a rattan chair and turned his face to the sky. "I'm glad the sun finally broke through! I need to catch a few rays."

"Got a crush on Bunni, have you?"

Tom shrugged. "She's okay."

Mac laughed. "You don't fool me." Taking a coin from his pocket, he handed it to Tom. "What do you think of this?" After Tom had studied it, Mac smiled. "That's an old counterfeit U.S. coin. Years ago some smooth operators made those coins right here in Ukee, then put them into boats and smuggled them across the border into Washington state."

"Is the U.S. that close?"

"It's not too long a trip in a good boat."

"Are these coins hard to make?"

"Not when you know how. Of course, those guys finally were captured. Then others decided to smuggle something different." From the pocket of his coat he produced an old bottle. "Rum."

"But can't Americans buy their own rum? Why smuggle it from Canada?"

"Decades ago in the United States they had some-thing called Prohibition. Nobody was allowed to sell any kind of alcohol. No whisky, no gin, no rum. But you could still buy it in Canada, so people smuggled booze across the border to sell to Americans who wanted to drink. Some handsome money was made around here." He paused, studying the bottle. "As a matter of fact, that's how Vernya's parents made their fortune."

"They were smugglers?"

"You bet. Now, don't tell that woman where you heard the story, but her folks were rum-runners for years. With the money they bought Nearby Island and built a resort over there. When they died the island was left to Vernya. She turned the resort into a fancy school for girls. They came from all over Canada, and even other countries, to live there and get an education. It was a good school, but then . . ."

"Then there was the accident! Please, Mac, tell me about it."

The man studied Tom's face, then shook his head. "Even though I'm not fond of Vernya, I won't talk about it. Nobody in this town will. It's bad luck. Besides, we had enough bad publicity at the time."

"But it's driving me crazy!"

"You're too curious for your own good, sonny." Mac raised a hand. "Now, how about a cup of tea and some fresh bread. Made it myself. You've never tasted anything finer."

Inside the house, Tom's mouth watered as Mac cut thick slices of brown bread, then spread butter and jam. "How long were you caretaker at the school?"

"I started working there before the . . . well . . . I stayed on after the school closed. Vernya wanted someone to guard the buildings so people wouldn't break in. I didn't get paid much, but Vernya gave me a cottage on the island and said I could retire there. She said I was like family . . ." Mac shook his head. "Anyway, then she tried to sell the school and finally got a company interested. But the law was changed, forcing places like hers to install a septic system instead of dumping raw sewage into the ocean. That would have been really expensive, so Vernya lost the sale. She was furious, especially since Nikki Vangelis lobbied hard to get the law passed."

"Maybe that's why they hate each other."

"I guess it's part of the reason." Mac poured steaming water into a tea pot, then led the way to the deck. "Since she can't sell the school, Vernya must be using up her savings pretty fast. I reckon she's nearly broke."

"So that's why she's logging the island."

"Vernya was a nice woman once. Then her parents died, and I guess she got lonely. She took a shine to Major Tosca, but he was already married. In the end he left his wife and married Vernya. That's when she turned strange and unpredictable. Shortly after, I was fired. She ordered me to leave the island and never return. Some way to treat family, huh?"

"Isn't there a caretaker looking after the deserted buildings now?"

Mac shook his head. "It isn't necessary. Everyone in Ukee has heard rumours about the ghost, so nobody goes near the place."

"Ghost? *What ghost?* Is there a spirit haunting the school? Was that the watery voice I heard last night?"

Mac sipped his tea in silence.

"Now I *have* to go back! Would you take me in your boat? Please, Mac?"

Tom expected Mac to refuse. But, to his surprise, the man nodded. "Okay, young fellow. Let's do that. I haven't been near the school since I was caretaker, and I'm kind of curious about those rumours, too. I'll run you to the island tonight, right after sunset, and let's see about that ghost." He rubbed Hogan's head. "We'll take along this fellow. He won't let any spirits attack us."

"Great!" Tom exclaimed. Quickly he drained his tea and then stood up. "And now I have to go. I've got . . . um . . . some reading to do."

As they followed the dog across the footbridge, Mac smiled at Tom. "I'll see you this evening. I'm looking forward to it. I could use some adventure in my life."

"Let's hope you don't get too much," Tom called over his shoulder as he headed toward the main road. Then he saw a car parked under some trees.

Behind the wheel sat Axe, staring at him.

* * *

The library was small and cozy. A young woman with curly hair and a friendly smile led Tom to the vertical file. "Here's what you're looking for. This contains lots of local stories taken from past issues of newspapers and magazines. Each one is in a separate file folder."

Tom carefully went through the vertical file, selecting items that sounded promising. If no one would tell him about the mysterious "accident" at the school, maybe he could find out for himself. He carried the files to the back of the library where there was a chair and a small desk with shelves for books and papers. Sitting down, he felt a surge of excitement as he opened the first file. Maybe this would produce results!

The file was marked "Tosca." It contained a number of clippings about both Major Tosca and his wife, Vernya. Most of the stories were about their many trips to London and Rome, but there was a long account of the grand opening of The Major's Galley. Tom was also interested to learn that Major Tosca had started a daily newspaper to serve Ucluelet and the nearby town of Tofino, but it had closed down after less than a year. In both instances a number of backers had lost quite a bit of money.

"Hey," Tom said to himself, "there's Mac." The man was shown in a photograph of the newspaper staff. "I wonder why Mac didn't tell me he once worked there?" Tom also recognized Major Tosca, Vernya and Axe. A few minutes later, in another photograph, Axe was seen beside an old-fashioned printing press. Above his head, a sign read "Tosca Print Shop," but the article explained that the print shop had been closed.

Tom reached for a file marked "Nearby Island." Inside he found a long magazine article with spectacular photographs from the air showing the mountain rising above the island's green forests. Tom studied the pictures, hoping to spot the secret hideout of Mosquito Joe, then he read the article. It was mostly about the island's wildlife, but Tom learned that Vernya had added several modern buildings when she converted the resort into a school. An old black-and-white picture showed the original resort, which was built on a slope rising from the ocean. Overlooking the water was a wooden lodge with a wide verandah, and a number of small cabins were scattered around the property. At the top of the slope was a large building with a bell tower. The story explained that dances had been held there.

Another article mentioned that Nearby Island was private property and not open to the public. As Tom thought about this, he opened a folded page of newspaper and whistled in surprise.

A large headline read "Tragedy at Nearby School." As Tom read the details, his body slowly turned cold. A young girl, a student at the school, had left a suicide note on her bed and gone into the forest. The next morning she'd been found, drowned in a stream.

"That voice," Tom whispered. "It sounded like a girl, calling from under water."

Again he read the article, refusing to believe his eyes. The story concluded with the information that the girl's father, a wealthy Calgary industrialist named Joseph Larson, blamed the school for his daughter's death.

Feeling dazed, Tom returned the files and left the library. Outside in the sunshine he shivered, thinking about the girl and the voice he'd heard. Suddenly he was not so anxious to return to Nearby Island, even with Mac and his dog for company.

Slowly Tom walked home, thinking about the day's events. Bunni lay in the yard in a white bikini, soaking up the sun while a radio blasted beside her head. Tom sprawled on the grass to tell her what he'd learned, but Bunni didn't seem interested. Going inside the house, he made a triple-decker sandwich and slumped down in front of the television set to watch the news.

There were items about bombings in the Middle East and fighting in Central America. Then the announcer began talking about a police investigation of a lottery-ticket scandal in Washington state. By chance, two people had showed up at the lottery office at exactly the same time to claim first prize, and each had a ticket with the winning number.

"One ticket was a counterfeit," the announcer said. "While office staff kept the two people talking, someone slipped into a back room to phone the police. Unfortunately the person with the counterfeit ticket panicked and ran from the office before police arrived. But a search has begun for the suspect, who is described as . . ."

At that moment Bunni came into the room and switched channels. "The news is so boring," she said, sitting down.

"Hey!" Tom shouted. Desperately he flicked the channels until he found the news again. But the announcer had begun an item about noise pollution on local lakes. "I wanted to write down that suspect's description."

"How come?"

"I keep files on people like that. Maybe I'll spot the counterfeiter on the street, and arrest him for the police."

"How do you know the counterfeiter is a man? It might be a woman."

"You're right, but now I'll never know. Too bad you switched channels."

"Yeah," Bunni said, yawning. Curling up on the sofa, she quickly became involved in a re-run of an old comedy show. Tom stared at her for a while, then settled back in his chair and tried to get involved in the program, too. It was time, he decided, to take a break from sleuthing.

* * *

Right after sunset, Tom received permission from Mr. and Mrs. Vangelis to visit Mac. Then he hurried toward the harbour. "I must ask him about the newspaper office. I'm surprised he didn't tell me about working for the Major."

By the time he reached the little house on stilts, the sky was already quite dark. Touches of colour reflected from the restless waters of the ocean, and Tom felt a prickle down his spine as he knocked on Mac's door.

There was no reply. Tom continued knocking, then cautiously opened the door. "Mac?" he called. "Are you home?"

Silence. A vein began to throb in Tom's throat. He tiptoed inside, staring at the empty room. Faint light came through the tall windows overlooking the harbour. Cautiously he moved forward, calling Mac's name, and then saw a piece of paper lying beside the CDs. Taking it to the window, he peered at the words. They had been written with the backward-slanting letters of a left-handed writer and were difficult to read. *Tom Austen*, the note said, *I cannot meet you tonight. Return home. Do not go to the school. It's dangerous. Mac.*

Tom looked out the window. Rocking in the waves at a nearby dock was Mac's orange boat. For a moment Tom hesitated. Then he quickly scrawled a message on the paper. *I've borrowed your boat. Hope it's okay. TA.*

A few minutes later he had started the motor and was heading out of the harbour. The boat was solid, but he was still jarred by every wave, and spray stung his face. A long, narrow channel led to the open sea, where a full moon was huge in the sky. Tom slowed the motorboat, thinking about the previous night when he'd gone to Nearby Island with Nikki. Which direction had she taken? He looked at a distant lighthouse, remembering its sweeping beam. Minutes later he recognized a second lighthouse, and knew he was following the correct route to the island.

The ocean seemed calmer tonight, and the full moon filled the sky with silver light. Looking over his shoulder, Tom studied the Big Dipper and other star formations, then gasped. A shooting star had blazed across the sky, showering stardust in its wake. "Another soul gone to heaven," Tom said, shivering. He wasn't superstitious like his sister, Liz, but he was sorry he hadn't made a wish before the shooting star died.

He thought about the girl who'd committed suicide at Nearby School. Had there been a shooting star when her soul went to heaven? Again he shivered, wishing he'd never found the newspaper article about the girl's death. It made investigating the school much more frightening, especially without Mac.

Where had Mac gone? Where was his dog? Why had he left a note, instead of phoning Tom at the Vangelis house? The questions tumbled in Tom's mind as the motorboat approached the looming black shape of Nearby Island. He thought of turning back, but couldn't. He had to find out what was happening on the island.

Tom kept the motorboat moving forward, listening to the noise of its engine echo from steep cliffs on the island. Somewhere in the night a seabird cried. A dark cloud crossed the moon, and then he saw the school.

The buildings rose on a slope overlooking the ocean. Tom recognized the ancient lodge he'd seen in the black-and-white photograph, and the building where dances had been held, but otherwise the scene had been changed by the addition of a number of modern buildings. Their walls were white, and large picture windows faced the ocean, some covered with plywood. Signs of decay were everywhere. Rust from a metal chimney stained one white wall, moss had spread over others, and small trees were growing between the steps of wooden porches.

By the shore, a boathouse extended over the waves, but there was no dock beside it. Moving slowly along the shore, Tom spotted the rickety remains of an old pier. Within minutes he had tied up the boat and was walking toward the school. His heart was thundering in his chest, and his legs shook. What was he doing here? Desperately he tried not to think about the girl who had drowned herself in the stream.

And then he heard the voice.

It cried out of the night, and it was terrible. Tom's mouth fell open and he moaned in horror as he listened to the watery voice. Over and over it called one terrible word—*beware . . . beware . . . beware*—while he shook with terror.

Then Tom ran. Swiftly, wildly, he raced toward the motorboat. Throwing off the lines, he leapt inside and gunned the engine. Giving the boat full throttle, he roared away from the dock. Waves smashed against the boat, soaking him with spray, but he could think of nothing but the terrible voice. He should never have returned to the school. He'd been a fool. On and on he raced until finally, far at sea, he slowed the boat and turned to look back.

In the distance the buildings of the deserted school gleamed under the moon, surrounded by the dark trees of the rainforest.

5

The next day a hot sun burned down from a cloudless sky. Tom sat in the yard beside Bunni, trying not to feel miserable.

He hadn't told anyone about racing in terror from the island. It was too embarrassing, especially now that the sunshine made his fears seem ridiculous. Still, he *had* heard the watery voice. It was real.

Bunni spread some lotion on her brown legs. "Nikki's given me her van for the day, and I'm going to Long Beach. Want to come?"

"Sure," Tom said. "When are you going?"

"In about an hour."

"Okay, I'll see you then. I've got something to do."

As he hurried down the hill to the harbour, Tom thought about all the things he wanted to ask Mac. He was pleased to find the man home. "I borrowed your boat last night," he said, as Mac prepared tea. "Was that okay?"

The man nodded.

"I went to the island."

Mac said nothing.

"Something terrible happened to me at the school."

Still Mac remained silent. After filling a tea pot, he led the way to the outdoor deck.

"Don't you want to know what happened?"

Mac didn't reply. Instead he sat down, sighing, and poured the tea.

"Too bad your dog's not around today," Tom said. "I miss him." Then he looked at Mac uneasily. "What went wrong, Mac? Why weren't you here last night?"

"Drink your tea, young fellow."

Tom studied the man's eyes. They seemed old today.

"I saw a picture of you, taken when you worked on the newspaper with Axe. How come you didn't tell me about that?"

Mac shrugged. "You didn't ask."

"But I couldn't! I didn't . . ."

Mac raised a hand, interrupting Tom. "Don't argue with me, young fellow. Not today."

"I'm sorry. I didn't mean to be rude."

"More tea?"

Tom shook his head. "I'm going to Long Beach with Bunni, so I'd better get home. Thanks for the tea." Mac just nodded, and Tom left, deeply puzzled. What was the matter with Mac?

Shortly after, Tom sat beside Bunni in the van as it headed north along the Tofino highway. The windows were open, music played, and Bunni looked great in designer sunglasses and a royal-blue cap which she wore low over her forehead. "What does the LAPD on your cap mean?" he asked.

"Los Angeles Police Department. A friend of mine got it down there, but I sweet-talked it out of him." Leaning on the horn, she passed a slow-moving car from New Brunswick. "One day I'll make it to California. I'd love to get into movies."

"You'd be fantastic, Bunni."

She flashed a smile his way. "Ever been to the movie studios down there?"

"Nope, but my sister has. She saw all the special effects demonstrated, like when they put blanks into a gun and pretend to shoot someone. The actor bites a capsule inside his mouth, and fake blood pours out. It's interesting, I guess, but I don't like knowing a show's all make-believe."

Minutes later Bunni turned off the highway and soon they reached a parking lot surrounded by trees. From the distance came the booming of surf. "I love Long Beach!" Bunni grinned at Tom. "I can't wait to show you."

A trail led down a steep bluff through the forest, and the rolling thunder of the surf grew louder. At last they reached the white sands of the beach, which stretched as far as Tom could see.

"It's fantastic!" Tom shielded his eyes against the sun as he gazed at the white breakers which rolled in to slam against the sand.

Within minutes they'd spread out beach towels and taken off their jeans and T-shirts. Glancing at Bunni's deep tan, which was set off perfectly by her white bikini, Tom hoped his own skin didn't look as pale as it felt. Trying to cheer up, he lay back and turned his face to the sun. For a few minutes he let the rays warm his body, then he sat up and looked around. Already he was bored, and Bunni's radio was playing terrible music. There were other people on the beach, but it was so enormous that he could hardly see the faces of even the nearest people—two children who were making a sand castle.

"I guess Japan is somewhere out there," he said, staring out to sea.

"Yup," Bunni mumbled sleepily. "People find glass Japanese fishing-net floats that wash up here after the ocean's carried them all the way across the Pacific. Personally, I'd rather they sent us some nice ghetto blasters."

Tom laughed. "Or maybe a Suzuki. That's the bike of my dreams."

"You know what Pacific Ocean means?"

"No."

"Peaceful ocean. I love the idea of someone naming an ocean for peace." Bunni shaded her eyes and looked at Tom. "Do you ever worry about nuclear war?"

"Yeah. A lot."

Bunni sat up. "Wouldn't it be neat if we could get the leaders from the United States and Russia to visit this beach with us? I bet if they just saw those little kids making their castle, they'd shake hands and agree to be friends."

"Sometimes I daydream about being prime minister and bringing peace to the world. Do you think I'm crazy?"

"Nope. I bet one day I'll see Prime Minister Austen on TV and I'll say, 'I once spent the day at Long Beach with him, talking peace.'" Bunni spread more lotion on her legs. Then she pointed at a rocky headland to the north. "I climbed up there once with this guy I know. We saw all the cormorants sitting on their nests with their faces to the cliff wall. Weird, eh? Andrew told me how crows steal their eggs. One of them approaches a cormorant, making a lot of noise to distract it, while a second crow sneaks up from behind and grabs the egg. Isn't that neat?"

Tom smiled. "Not if you're a cormorant."

"Andrew once travelled all the way to a marsh near Vancouver so he could see a spoonbill sandpiper that had wandered there from Asia by mistake. He's crazy about birds."

I'm crazy about you, Tom felt like saying, but instead he lifted his face to the wind, sniffed the salty sea air like a cat, then stretched luxuriously. At that moment the mysterious voice on Nearby Island seemed light years away.

"Ever wonder who you'll marry, Bunni?"

"Sure."

"Sometimes I think about the girl I'll marry. I wonder where she lives and what she's doing at this very moment." Tom laughed. "I keep telling you all my secrets."

"My sister was married once, and she wasn't too impressed with it. I guess she had a bad experience, but I'll still risk it. I've already got my wedding planned, right down to the pink Cadillac and the number of layers on my cake. Then I want a big house at the Point. That's where Vernya and her husband live, in a really fancy place. They had an old house in town, but it burned down. Nikki thinks the fire was deliberately set, so Vernya could collect the insurance."

"Boy, your sister really doesn't think much of Vernya, does she?"

Bunni shrugged. "She has her reasons." Then she suddenly sat up, shielding her eyes. "Well, speak of the devil. Here comes Vernya now."

Tom looked across the beach at the woman and her husband, who were strolling their way holding hands.

"Hi, there!" Major Tosca said. "Isn't this weather perfect? I shouldn't reveal the secrets of Ukee, Tom, but we don't always have sunshine. Sometimes big drops of water fall from the sky."

Vernya laughed. "We just call it liquid sunshine." She smiled at Bunni. "You and the Major both have wonderful tans. Too bad I'm a redhead like Tom. In this rainy climate, the best I can hope for is to rust prettily." She winked at Tom, who blushed and stared at the sandpipers running along the wet sand close to the pounding surf. Vernya could really be very nice. For some reason it made him feel guilty to know that Nikki disliked her so much. It almost made him feel disloyal or something.

The Major offered a cigarette to Vernya, but she shook her head. "I'm trying to give them up."

Tom smiled. "I finally convinced my mom to quit smoking, but it was hard work. You know how I finally got through to her? For my last birthday I said there was only one present I wanted, and that was for her to throw every cigarette in the garbage can."

"She must love having a son like you."

Tom grinned. "Except when she has to drive me to hockey practice at five in the morning. Do you have any kids?"

Vernya shook her head. Then she took Bunni's arm. "Why don't you two join us for a stroll on the beach?" As they started walking, Tom fell into step beside Major Tosca, watching the seagulls swooping and dipping in the wind.

"I guess they're always looking for fish," Tom said. "Do you like to fish, Major?"

The man hesitated, then shook his head. "When I was your age I loved to fish," he said in a low voice. "Then one day when my family was on holiday in New Westminster, my brother and I went fishing at the river. We'd been told to stay away, but we wanted to fish, so we went anyway. The pier was wet from rain, and my brother slipped. He fell into the river."

For a moment the Major was silent.

"Billy managed to grab a piling. The current was very strong. I reached for him but . . . I wasn't strong enough to hold him. The . . . the river tore him away."

A pulse was beating in Tom's throat. "What happened to him?"

"He drowned." Major Tosca shook his head. "Since that day I've never really been comfortable around water."

Silently Tom trudged across the sand beside Major Tosca. They caught up to Vernya and Bunni just as they reached an outcropping that jutted into the sea. Far offshore the water looked calm, but Tom could see where waves began to curl over to form huge white breakers. They came foaming in, churning the water around the rocks into a pale green, whirling and roaring and leaping into the air. There was tremendous power in the water, even on a calm day.

"Do boats ever get wrecked around here?"

"You bet." Major Tosca pointed to the south. "Somewhere down there is the West Coast Trail. People hike it these days, but a century ago the natives used the trail to help sailors reach safety after they'd been shipwrecked. Many lives have been lost along this coast. They call it the Graveyard of the Pacific. The passenger liner *Valencia* was probably the worst disaster. It went down in 1906."

"What happened?"

"The ship came up the coast from San Francisco. Around midnight, in rough weather, it missed the entrance to the strait and ran up on the rocks. Some people managed to get ashore, and eventually rescue boats appeared from Victoria. But the seas were so heavy the rescuers could just watch as people waved for help from the rigging, or leapt into the sea hoping to swim ashore. There were 136 drowned." Major Tosca shuddered. "It must have been horrible."

"I'm glad those things don't happen today."

"Don't bet on it. Early this year a Japanese freighter went down with its load of cars near here. It lost its way and ran straight into the rocks just like the *Valencia*." Major Tosca looked grimly at the waves foaming around the outcropping.

The sun was hot on their backs as they wandered back along the beach. Far in the distance, where the sand met the forest, lay jumbled heaps of log bleached white by rain and sun. Tom realized they'd been thrown there by winter storms.

The Major was walking along the beach alone, lost in thought. Bunni was already heading back to where she and Tom had left their towels and radio.

"Look at this, Tom." Vernya reached into the green water of a shallow tidal pool and lifted out a snail shell. To Tom's surprise, the shell began darting around her hand. "It's a hermit crab," she said, smiling. She turned over the shell to reveal the crab's tiny legs, pumping furiously, then gently placed it back in the water. "When the baby hermit outgrows its shell, it will find another one to live in."

Tom looked at Vernya closely. "May I ask you something?"

"Sure."

"Isn't there any way to save your island? I feel sick when I think of it being logged."

To Tom's surprise, tears rose in Vernya's eyes. Then she shook her head. "The island will be logged. Work has already begun, so there's nothing to discuss."

"When I flew out from Winnipeg it was horrible to look down from the plane. The forests were like velvet, running up the slopes of the mountains, but there were all these logging scars. It looked like a person's head with hair torn out in patches."

"Drop it, Tom. I'm tired of the subject."

Nothing more was said until they reached Bunni. The news was being broadcast on the radio. "Hey, listen," Tom said. "They're saying something about Nearby Island!"

". . . the injunction granted today will last until the

native land question is settled," the announcer said. "This process could take several years. In the meantime, the court has ordered all logging on Nearby Island to stop immediately. No more trees can be cut until the question of ownership is decided."

As the announcer went on to an item about the price of oil, Major Tosca stared in horror at the radio. Then he turned to his wife. An instant before, a smile had appeared on her face, but now she looked furious.

"They can't stop the logging!" she hissed. "I won't let it happen."

Tom watched Vernya and her husband hurry away across the beach. "What do you think they'll do now?"

"I don't know. Logging the island was their last chance for money. Everyone knows they owe the banks for a bunch of loans. Now Vernya will lose the Lotus and that beautiful house. At the very least."

"Maybe they'll fight the injunction. Take it to the Supreme Court in Ottawa, or something like that."

Bunni shook her head. "I don't know, but I'll bet Vernya does something. She's a real fighter."

"Well, it's great the island has been saved. Nikki's going to be happy about that."

But when they reached home they found Nikki slumped in a lawn chair, listening to the radio as news of the court injunction was repeated. Switching it off, she lifted a hand in a vague greeting. "Have you heard?"

"Yes," Bunni replied. "We happened to be with the Toscas when we got the news. Vernya was spitting mad."

Tom smiled at Nikki. "You must be glad the logging has been stopped."

She shook her head. "I'd like to be, but I don't trust Vernya. She won't let this stop her. I just know it."

"Come on, Nikki," Bunni coaxed. "Forget about Vernya for once. The logging has stopped. You've won."

"No, I haven't," Nikki muttered. "Not yet."

* * *

It was two days before the Toscas were mentioned again. That afternoon, Nikki rushed into the house as Tom and Bunni were washing the lunch dishes.

"Have you heard?" she said breathlessly. "Vernya and Warwick are leaving town. Permanently."

"What?"

"It's true. Their house is being sold, and they're sailing tomorrow on the *Lady Rose*."

"What's the *Lady Rose*?"

"It's a boat that was built in Scotland decades ago. It leaves Port Alberni in the morning for here, stopping at fishing villages along the way to drop cargo and passengers. Later in the day it heads home from Ukee."

"Why don't the Toscas just drive to Port Alberni? There's a highway."

"That's a good question, Tom. I think Vernya's up to something, and I wish I knew what it was."

"Hey," Tom said. "Why don't we go along on the *Lady Rose*? That way we could keep an eye on them."

Nikki thought for a moment and then smiled slowly. "Sure, why not? Besides, Tom, it's part of your tourist's education. The *Lady Rose* is a legend around here."

Bunni opened her mouth to protest, and then threw her dish towel in the sink in exasperation. "Well, then, I'm coming, too. You guys need a watchdog."

Later that afternoon, Tom took a walk through town. As he strolled in the hot sunshine, he saw Mac approach, looking depressed. When he heard about the Toscas leaving town, he exploded.

"Those liars! Those double-crossers!" Mac rubbed angrily at the bristles on his chin, then slammed his hands together. "Now it all fits together. I saw Axe this morning, and he was furious. Vernya and the Major just fired him. They gave him two weeks' pay and told him to find another job. After all his years of faithful service. And now I've been betrayed again, too." Mac narrowed his eyes and muttered hoarsely, "Somebody should take care of that woman."

6

The next day, Tom left the house early. He couldn't wait to catch his first glimpse of the *Lady Rose*.

The freighter was much smaller than he'd expected. Its black funnel and white wheelhouse rose barely higher than the dock, and Tom wondered briefly if this was the correct boat. Where would the passengers sit? But on the hull a carved wooden sign read *Lady Rose*, and he could see passenger benches under a canvas canopy at the stern. Forward of the benches was an enclosed area with stairs leading down, perhaps to a cabin below decks.

The shrill whine of machinery sounded from near the wheelhouse, where a surprisingly young captain was supervising the loading of cargo. Tom watched as a pallet on the dock was loaded with haversacks and food and other camping supplies, then winched aboard and lowered into the hold. Next to be loaded was a rubber Zodiac with a 100-horsepower outboard engine that looked capable of pushing the small craft through even the roughest seas.

Beside Tom was a distinguished-looking man with a white moustache. A hearing aid was visible in his ear. "Wonderful town you've got here," he said, smiling at Tom. "I'm a tourist myself, from the great state of Wisconsin. Tell me, where's this freighter bound?"

As Tom talked about the *Lady Rose*, he felt proud to be taken for a local. In a short time he'd grown to love Ukee, and he felt a warm glow as he looked at the colourful wooden houses crowding the hill above the harbour. A seagull circling high above gave a piercing cry, while the low throb of a gillnetter's engine sounded across the water as it headed out to sea.

For a while Tom watched a young woman take pictures of everything in sight with a 35-millimetre camera. Then he followed a ramp down to a lower dock. Here he discovered scores of fishboats, and spent time studying their nets and fluorescent buoys and tall masts reflected in the shimmering water.

In the distance, far down the harbour, was Mac's house, but there was no sign of life. As Tom returned to the upper dock, he received a shock.

Staring at him with narrowed eyes was Axe.

"Oh . . . um . . . hi, there." Tom scrambled for something to say. The man was so big, and his eyes were angry. "Are you going on the *Lady Rose*, too?"

"I don't like double-crossers." Axe stared at a taxi arriving on the dock. Inside were Vernya and her husband. The big man said nothing more as the Toscas got out of the taxi. Ignoring Axe, they collected their suitcases and went on board the *Lady Rose*. The moment they disappeared down the stairs, Axe followed.

Tom was also about to follow when a horn tooted. He saw Nikki's van approaching. She climbed out with Bunni. Then they kissed their parents and watched them drive away. "Mom and Dad will collect us in Port Alberni," Nikki said.

"*If* we survive the journey," said Bunni. "Please, Nikki, stay away from Vernya. Otherwise there'll be fireworks, I just know it."

"Stop worrying."

Tom followed them across the dock to a wooden gangplank that led to the deck of the *Lady Rose*. As he stepped onto the freighter, he felt an ominous sense of foreboding.

Maybe this trip had not been such a good idea after all.

Tom walked toward the stern, looking in the windows of a small cabin in the centre of the freighter and then glancing at a lifeboat by the railing. At the stern a Canadian flag flapped in the wind. Tom looked down at the cold water, then heard the whine of machinery and turned to see the gangplank being winched aboard. The *Lady Rose* was about to set sail!

He hurried forward as workers on the dock released the boat's large hawsers, freeing the freighter. It drifted away from the dock. Then the ship vibrated as power was fed to the propeller. Whistle blasting, the *Lady Rose* headed toward mid-channel while people on the dock waved goodbye.

A cool breeze ruffled Tom's clothes, making him glad the afternoon sun was hot. He sat on a wooden chest and put his feet on a chain that ran along the side of the boat.

As the *Lady Rose* left Ucluelet, people waved from the decks of fishing boats moored at the town's wharves and fish-packing plants. For a short time, as the freighter steamed along the inlet, there was a good view of the nearby shore, where tall trees stood above beaches littered with logs and smooth grey boulders. Then the *Lady Rose* began to encounter rolling swells. As waves foamed away from its hull, the freighter entered the open ocean. Here everything was blue: the vast sparkling sea, the perfect sky above—even the distant islands wreathed in blue mists.

"Wow," Tom said, as Bunni joined him. "I wouldn't have missed this for the world." Shading his eyes, he tried to find Nearby Island. "Isn't that it, with the mountain?"

"Yup."

Tom shivered, remembering the ghostly voice he'd heard. Maybe, when he got back to Ukee, he'd find the courage to visit the school once more. Somehow he had to learn more about that voice.

Turning, Tom studied the other passengers on the deck. Nearby was a young couple accompanied by an older man who smiled hesitantly at Tom before again looking out to sea. Two women who had wheeled bicycles on board at Ucluelet were eating apples and talking together with accents that sounded Texan, while a blond man in a UBC sweatshirt was patting his dog, which gripped a Frisbee in its teeth.

Suddenly the freighter's speed dropped. People rushed to the railing to watch as a small boat came speeding across the blue sea. The words *Gerry's Taxi* were written on its hull, and a pretty woman sat at the outboard motor in its stern. But it was the man in the bow that Tom stared at.

"It's Mac!"

As the water taxi slipped into the shadow of the freighter, Tom leaned over the railing to watch. Directly below was a cargo door close to the water line. The moment the taxi bumped against the *Lady Rose,* Mac climbed through the cargo door and the woman gunned the outboard. The taxi flashed away, leaving behind a bubbling white wake.

"I'm going below," Tom said. "I want to find out why Mac is here."

"I'll come with you. There's a coffee shop down there."

The narrow stairs led down to a cabin which smelled faintly of diesel oil. Sunlight came through the portholes, showing wooden benches where passengers were reading or playing cards. Tom saw Mac about to sit down, and went to join him.

"Mac! Boy, is this a surprise!"

"I decided to get some sea air."

"Why didn't you board in Ukee?"

The man shrugged. "It was a . . . last-minute decision. I saw the *Lady Rose* steam past my place, heading for the open sea, so I phoned Gerry and she collected me in the water taxi."

"Are you joining the Toscas? Is that why you're here?"

"You ask a lot of questions. Are you just a nosy kid, or are you writing a book?"

"Sorry, sir," Tom mumbled. Mac sure had changed. What was the matter with him, anyway? Tom sighed and turned to Bunni. "Did you say there's a coffee shop? I'm kind of hungry."

"It's this way."

They walked along a corridor past a steel bulkhead which throbbed with the sound of the ship's engine, and then entered the coffee shop. Hamburgers sizzled on a stove, and a few passengers sat at tables. Major Tosca and Vernya leaned over one, talking intently, while Axe sat in a corner watching them with narrowed eyes. In the other corner was Nikki, who waved them to her table.

"Enjoying the trip, Tom?"

"You bet. The sea air's given me an appetite. I think I'll stock up."

"Try the flapjacks. They're the best in the west."

Tom gave his order to the cook and returned to the table. Sealed beneath its plastic surface was a chart of Barkley Sound, showing the route of the *Lady Rose*. Tom studied it, then looked at the table's raised wooden edge. "What's this for?"

"To keep plates and cutlery from sliding off during heavy seas."

"But this water's calmer than my bathtub."

"Storms blow up fast on the west coast."

Tom's mouth watered as the cook brought him a plate of steaming flapjacks, three-high. A large blob of yellow butter was melting on top, and twisted pieces of crisp bacon were arranged around the plate. He dug in, concentrating all his attention on the food until the plate was empty and his stomach groaned. Then, sighing deeply, he leaned back from the table. "Did you know Mac came on board?"

Nikki nodded and pointed at a door. "After Mac climbed from the water taxi into the hold he passed through here on his way to the passenger cabin."

"Are we allowed to see the hold?"

"Sure."

A short passage led to the hold. Tom recognized the rubber Zodiac that had been loaded at Ucluelet, and the pallet with the camping supplies. Cartons of food for the coffee shop were stacked near a red canoe, and hawsers hung in big loops on the steel hull. From below the deck came the rushing sound of water.

"Hey!" Tom pointed toward the open cargo door. "Are we ever close to shore." Outside the door, darkly shadowed evergreens looked near enough to touch, and Tom could practically count the barnacles on the rocks.

"We're sailing through the Broken Group Islands," Nikki said. "There's about one hundred of them clustered together here, most of them tiny. The *Lady Rose* will be stopping soon at Gibraltar Island. Let's go above to watch."

The *Lady Rose* had dropped its speed and was following a passage that seemed no wider than a city street. To one side was the thick forest of a small island, while to the other was a small cove with a pebbly beach.

Tom leaned over the railing to watch the *Lady Rose* thread its way among the islands. The water was green here and seemed as peaceful as a lake, but drifting strands of kelp were a reminder that they were still on the Pacific. Seagulls floated in packs enjoying the warm sunshine as the *Lady Rose* approached a wooden float anchored in the cove.

"This is Gibraltar Island," Nikki said. "The Broken Group is part of Pacific Rim National Park. Lots of people come to these islands to kayak and scuba-dive and bird-watch. It looks like we're picking up some campers for the trip to Port Alberni."

People waited on the float, surrounded by camping supplies and canoes. As soon as the *Lady Rose* was made fast, they began handing their equipment through the cargo door to the ship's crew. Watching from the bridge was the *Lady Rose*'s young captain, who glanced in Tom's direction and then smiled broadly. Leaving the bridge, he hurried toward him.

"Hi there! Welcome aboard!"

Tom mumbled a reply before realizing that the captain was greeting Nikki and Bunni, who seemed to be old friends. Then Tom was introduced. "Come to the bridge later for a visit, Tom." The captain leaned over the railing to check progress at the hold, then looked at his watch. "I'm getting worried. We're already running late, and we have to make an unscheduled side-trip that will cost us time."

"Where are we going?" Nikki asked.

"Effingham Inlet. One of the houseboat people who lives up there is ill. We're taking him to hospital in Port Alberni."

"I don't care if we're late," Tom said. "This is a great trip, and I wouldn't mind some extra time. The weather is fabulous."

"Actually, the weather is exactly what worries me."

"What do you mean?"

"The barometer is dropping fast. We're going to be hit by a storm."

"A real one?"

The captain nodded, frowning. "Yes. It's going to be very bad indeed."

7

A salmon leapt clear of the sea.

Its body flashed silver in the sun. Then it smacked back to the surface and was gone again into the depths. Tom caught his breath. "Did you see that, Bunni?"

She nodded. "Sometimes I wonder if they do that to feed, or just for the thrill of powering up through the water to fly into the air."

"Probably both," Nikki said.

Tom sat on deck with the two sisters. The *Lady Rose* was steaming under full power in a bid to outrun the coming storm. He still found it difficult to believe that bad weather was on its way. The sunlight danced on the ocean, waves rolled away from the hull with a constant liquid sound, and the sea air was delicious. In a sheltered cove Tom could see a fishboat shining white against the dark shadows of the forest. Above the cove was the rich texture of the trees climbing a steep mountainside to the blue sky.

Then Major Tosca and his wife appeared on deck, holding hands, and Tom could immediately feel Nikki tense. She pretended to ignore the couple as they cuddled together at the railing, but the creases between her eyes deepened. Then she suddenly pointed to shore and yelled.

"Do you see that, Vernya? Your island would look like that!"

On a nearby slope all the forest had been logged away. Only rock and bare soil and dead trees remained, along with abandoned logging roads which cut the mountainside like knife slashes.

"That's awful," Tom muttered. "It's like a giant shark took a bite out of the mountain. There's nothing left."

Bunni stared at the devastation. "I didn't know it was that bad. Those dead trees look like a game of pickup sticks. Why don't the companies use them?"

"There's terrible waste in logging," Nikki answered. "They take the valuable trees and leave the rest to rot. The companies claim it would cost too much to transport them to market, but that's just an excuse for poor forest management. It makes me furious."

"What can we do?" Tom said.

"Get everyone in your class at school to write the government asking for stronger regulation of forest companies."

"Does the government care what kids think?"

"Of course! In a few years you'll be able to vote.

This is your country, Tom, and you kids should get involved now in saving it from things like that logging mess. Not to mention acid rain and wolf kills." For a moment Nikki was silent, but her body was rigid with anger as she stared at Vernya.

"Don't fight the injunction, Vernya. Leave the island in peace."

"I'm not fighting it. I accept the court's decision."

"I don't believe you. I think you're going to Port Alberni to sweet-talk the judge into overturning the injunction."

Vernya laughed.

Major Tosca put a stick of gum in his mouth and dropped the wrapper overboard. "Those old cedars on Nearby Island need to be logged. Otherwise they'll just get overmature, and that doesn't help anyone."

Nikki stared at him. "Sometimes, Warwick, you say the dumbest things. Do you think the whole forest is going to collapse into a heap if it's not logged?"

"Could be."

"That's so absurd," Nikki said. Then she pointed at the package of gum in his hand. "Anyway, you shouldn't drop litter in the ocean. Everyone knows that."

"The wrapper will sink."

"Sure, but there's a principle involved. Other people with the same attitude own tankers that are cleaned at sea. They dump oil into the ocean and think nothing of it."

Major Tosca shook his head. "Honestly, you Greenpeacers will get excited about anything. You know, Nikki, maybe we should fight that injunction. It would be fun to watch you get steamed up."

"If you try it, I'll stop you. I mean that. *I will stop you.*"

* * *

Three hours later, the storm struck.

The *Lady Rose* was still far from Port Alberni because of the time spent at Effingham Inlet waiting for the sick person to be brought by skiff from his houseboat. Finally, after he'd been safely installed in one of the tiny cabins below decks, the freighter headed into the heavy swells and strong winds of the storm.

Tom stood at the bow, gripping the steel railing as he leaned into the wind. Gulls shrieked and tumbled above his head, loving the storm. The only other passenger on deck was the woman with the camera, who was leaning out over the sea to get artistic shots of the white waves leaping away from the hull. Then she, too, went below and Tom was left alone on deck.

Finally, as night fell and his hands turned blue with cold, Tom also went below. Down in the cabin, he found that the storm had affected many of the passengers. Some lay on the benches, groaning each time the ship slammed into a wave, while others huddled together in the dim light. Nikki and Bunni seemed fine, and so did Axe and Mac, who both sat motionless in different corners of the cabin. But Vernya was pale and her husband was in terrible shape. Sweat shone on his forehead, his skin looked like wax, and his eyes stared from his face.

"How is it above?" he said to Tom in a weak voice.

"Could you see Port Alberni?"

"No, Major. It's dark out now, but I couldn't see any lights ahead."

"We're going to drown." He stared at his wife. "We should never have decided on this."

"It's too late to turn back now," she replied.

Then suddenly the lights went out.

Someone screamed, and Major Tosca shouted. The ship rolled, throwing Tom off balance. He lurched forward, hands desperately clawing at the black air for support. Voices cried out, there was more screaming, and then Nikki managed to make herself heard about the din.

"Calm down! The cabin lights have failed, but we're perfectly safe. I'm going for a storm lantern. I'll be right back."

The strength in Nikki's voice seemed to have a calming effect. The shouts and screams stopped, although moans could still be heard. Tom pulled himself up on a bench, trying not to feel sick as the *Lady Rose* rolled back and forth through the heavy seas.

At last a yellow glow appeared in the corridor leading from the coffee shop. Nikki emerged holding a small lantern which spluttered and hissed as it threw dancing shadows on her face. "It's pretty weak," she said, hanging the lantern from a hook, "but it'll have to do."

Tom turned to study the cabin. Axe still watched Vernya with narrowed eyes, and Mac sat with the same glum expression on his face.

"Major Tosca!" Tom exclaimed. "Where is he?"

Nikki stared at the bench where Vernya's husband

had been sitting, then turned to the stairs. "He may have gone above. I'd better see."

"I'll go with you."

Nikki and Tom hurried up the stairs, where they had to force open the door against the wind which buffeted it from outside. Above their heads the wires of the rigging vibrated and shrieked. "The weather's improving!" Nikki shouted into Tom's ear. "The storm's not as bad."

"You've got to be joking!"

A spotlight on the bulkhead shone on Nikki's face and showed her long brown hair whipping in the wind. "There he is," she shouted, pointing toward the railing. "I'll bet he never travels by sea again."

The man leaned over the railing, back and shoulders heaving. "He shouldn't have thrown that gum wrapper overboard," Tom said. "The sea's revenge against litterbugs is truly awesome."

Nikki grinned. "I'm going below."

"I'm not! I love it up here." Reeling and swaying, Tom struggled across the deck. Grabbing a stanchion, he held tight as the wind ripped and tore at his clothes. From somewhere close by came the sound of a motor. Amazed at the courage of anyone who would brave this weather, Tom shielded his eyes trying to find the boat in the darkness. Then he saw the lights shining from the wheelhouse and remembered the captain's invitation to visit the bridge.

Fighting his way forward, he pounded on the wheelhouse door and was taken inside by a surprised captain. "You're one brave kid," the man said, smiling. "I'm sure everyone else is below decks feeling as if they're about to die."

Tom watched, fascinated, as the captain concentrated on the freighter's battle with the sea. Glowing lights from various instruments shone on his bearded face as he leaned close to the window, giving instructions to the crew member at the wheel. Another person was with them, but Tom couldn't make out his face in the dim light.

"Still enjoying the trip?" the captain asked, smiling.

"It's fantastic. I was at the bow until I got too cold."

"I saw you there."

"Is this the worst storm you've been in?"

The captain shook his head. "Some winters we've been hit by hurricane-force winds. I've seen waves higher than telephone poles. At times I've felt nervous, but the *Lady Rose* is solid and dependable. She's even survived a tidal wave."

"Wow! What happened?"

"You've probably seen maps of this area, so you'll know Alberni Inlet is very long and narrow. It was carved out by a glacier millenniums ago. One year a major earthquake in Alaska sent a massive swell across the Pacific. When it reached Alberni Inlet, the swell was squeezed between the narrow rocky walls as it roared up to Port Alberni. It smashed into the city, causing a lot of damage, but this good old beauty just rode it out."

The pride in the man's voice made Tom feel good.

"Why are the deck spotlights still working, when the power failed in the passenger cabin?" he asked.

"Two separate electrical systems."

Tom smiled. "Well, I'd better get below. Thanks for the visit."

"You're welcome. Come for another sea voyage, next time you're out from Winnipeg."

"Will do!"

Leaving the warmth of the wheelhouse, Tom was immediately battered by the wind. He struggled along the deck, gripping the rail for support. The shriek of the rigging wires high above was a frightening sound, like the ghosts of shipwrecked sailors wailing in misery. Would the *Lady Rose* also go to a watery grave? It didn't seem possible with such a brave captain in control, but the thought still made Tom nervous, and he was glad to reach the door that led below.

Then he saw Vernya.

She stood at the stern, hands tight on the railing. Her face, which was turned in Tom's direction, was lit by a spotlight. Her mouth was open and she seemed to be crying out, but the wind tore away her words and whirled them into the night.

Turning from the doorway, Tom fought his way along the heaving deck toward Vernya. He called her name, but no sound could be heard in the terrible night. Reaching the cluster of benches near the stern, he stepped into the glow of a spotlight and waved his arm to attract Vernya's attention.

She saw Tom and shouted something, perhaps a warning, then pointed toward a lifeboat. Someone was crouched on its far side with only feet and legs visible. Tom stared in horror as a hand appeared, holding a gun.

It was aimed at Vernya.

As the person squeezed the trigger, flame leapt from the muzzle. Shocked, Tom swung toward Vernya. She clutched her stomach and blood spurted from her mouth. He took a step toward her, one hand outstretched, and then heard another shot.

Vernya staggered into the railing, tried desperately to clutch it, and then fell backwards into the night. Suddenly she was gone, leaving only the darkness and the howling wind.

8

For a long moment Tom was frozen by shock.

Then he stumbled forward. Reaching the rail he stared into the darkness but could see nothing. Spray lashed his face. The wind threatened to tear him loose from the freighter and plunge him into the raging sea.

"The captain! He's got to stop the ship!"

Tom started forward, then remembered the person behind the lifeboat. He looked fearfully that way, but could see no one. He struggled on into the wind. His entire body was numb, and his legs could hardly function. At long last he reached the wheelhouse door. Pulling it open, he staggered inside to gasp out his story.

The horrified captain ordered the crew to rescue stations, but little could be done. "If those shots didn't kill her," he said at last to Tom, "then she's certainly drowned. We'll have to carry on to Port Alberni and hope that her body can be found after the storm dies down. I've noted our position in the ship's log and radioed the RCMP to be waiting for us on arrival."

As the *Lady Rose* got under way again, Tom left the wheelhouse for the passenger cabin below decks. Word of Vernya's fate had reached the others, who sat silently in the faint light of small candles. It was difficult to see their expressions, but Tom could sense their shock. *Who had fired the gun?* Tom was sure it had been someone with a personal connection to Vernya.

He sat down beside Nikki and Bunni. Nikki sat hunched forward as though a great weight was on her shoulders. Bunni watched her sister with eyes that looked badly frightened. Neither spoke as Tom joined them.

"Are you okay?" he asked.

Nikki took his hand. Her fingers were cold. "Wasn't there anything you could do?"

He shook his head. "It happened so quickly."

"Yes," she whispered. "I'm sure it was over in a flash. Thank goodness for that. I feel so terrible."

Tom studied Nikki's face, remembering how much she'd disliked Vernya. Why was she taking the woman's death so hard? Then he looked at the candles flickering around the cabin. "Those weren't here before. What happened to the storm lantern?"

"Vernya broke it," Bunni explained. "After you left the cabin she seemed to get very upset. She paced up and down and then suddenly grabbed the storm lantern from its hook. She started toward the stairs and slipped. As she fell, she dropped the lantern. It smashed on the deck and went out."

"So everything was dark?"

Bunni nodded. "There were screams and shouts, the same as earlier, but Nikki had a lot more trouble getting people calmed down. Then she had to find a crew member who could help, and we all sat in the dark for a long time. Eventually Nikki came back with the candles. That was when the boat stopped. A little while later we heard from a crew member what had happened to Vernya."

"When did Vernya leave the cabin?"

Bunni shrugged. "I don't know. Everything was dark for so long."

"Did the darkness last long enough for someone to go above, shoot Vernya, and come back to this cabin without being seen?"

"Yup."

"You said Vernya was upset. Could you tell why?"

Bunni shook her head. "I thought she was worried about her husband, throwing up over the rail. I figured she went above to see if he was all right."

Tom sighed. "The police will have trouble sorting out this mess." He looked across the cabin at Mac, who seemed unchanged by the tragedy, and then at Major Tosca, whose face sagged under the stress of an unknown emotion. Despair? Grief? Fear?

Then he noticed Axe.

The man looked terrified. His eyes darted from passenger to passenger, while his arms tightly clenched his body. When he noticed Tom watching him, his eyes dropped. For several seconds he stared at the deck, then glanced again at Tom. His forehead was damp with perspiration, and he licked at his dry lips.

Then Axe stood up. Swiftly he moved toward the forward corridor. "Where do you think he's going?" Tom whispered to Bunni.

"Probably to the head."

"What's that?"

"It's a fancy word used on ships. It means the washroom."

"Oh."

Tom watched the corridor carefully, waiting for Axe to come back. But nothing happened, and at last he stood up. "I'll be right back." He walked quickly to the corridor. Finding no sign of the man in the head, he went on to the coffee shop. The cook and another crew member sat at a table, playing cards by the light of a storm lantern.

"Did anyone go through here?"

"Just that big guy—the one who looks like a tank. He was heading for the hold."

Tom hurried on, certain now that something was wrong. Opening the door into the hold, he heard the rushing sound of the sea air pouring in through the open cargo door. Lights shone inside the hold, showing the cartons of food and the camping supplies and canoes.

But the Zodiac was gone.

Tom stared at the empty space where the rubber craft had been, then rushed across the deck to the cargo door. The light from the hold was bright enough to show the outline of the Zodiac, escaping into the night through the spray-flecked waves of the frenzied sea. Alone in the stern of the little craft was Axe.

* * *

The Mounties were waiting at the dock when the *Lady Rose* reached Port Alberni. Many hours passed as they questioned the captain, crew and passengers. A police dog was brought on board to search for the gun but found nothing. It seemed likely that it had been thrown overboard immediately after the shots had been fired.

Finally the passengers were released. The dock lights reflected from puddles of rainwater left behind by the storm, which had moved on across Vancouver Island. Bright stars shone above, and columns of steam rose into the night sky from the pulp-and-paper mill dominating the community.

Taxis were waiting to transport the passengers to a motel. Everyone had been instructed by the RCMP to remain in the town while the investigation continued— a process that might take days.

"I don't mind," Tom said, yawning in the back seat of a taxi. "I could sleep for days, or maybe weeks."

Bunni didn't answer. She looked out at the passing streets, deserted at this hour, then turned anxious eyes to her sister. Nikki had hardly spoken for hours, except to answer the Mounties' questions, and there were dark lines under her eyes. She said nothing until everyone had been assigned rooms at the motel. Then, as Tom took his key from the desk clerk and started toward his room, she grabbed his arm.

"You're absolutely certain she went overboard?"

"Yes, Nikki. You asked me that already."

Bunni took her sister's arm. "Come on, Nik," she said quietly. "Let's go. I'll run a bath for you."

Tom headed for his room and fell on the bed. His body still seemed to be tossing with the motion of the waves, and he had a sudden vision of the ghosts of sailors dancing in the rigging of the *Lady Rose*. The vision turned into a dream, and he slept.

Several days passed as the RCMP investigation continued. When not being questioned, Tom wandered around town. He sat on the docks watching raw logs and the mill's wood products being loaded onto freighters with foreign names, or staring at pleasure boats fishing the inlet for salmon. Once Bunni went with him, but she went back to the motel early to be with Nikki.

Every day Tom tried to figure out the puzzle of Vernya's murder. Who was responsible? Why had Axe left the *Lady Rose* in such a hurry, and where was he now? Tom had told the police about Axe's sudden departure, but the man hadn't been found yet.

Tom spent hours sitting in the motel lobby watching Major Tosca, Mac and the others as they passed by. Major Tosca seemed to be very preoccupied. He kept asking for messages at the motel's front desk. He didn't seem particularly grief-stricken, Tom thought, but maybe he had a lot on his mind, settling Vernya's affairs and whatever. Mac hardly spoke to anyone and spent most of his time in his room.

Then, on his fourth night in Port Alberni, the ringing phone woke Tom from a deep sleep. Reaching out blindly, he knocked over the bedside lamp and a glass of water before he could find the phone in the darkness and lift the receiver.

"Yes?" he mumbled. "Who is it?"

There was no answer. He could hear someone breathing at the other end, but nothing else.

Instantly Tom was wide awake. "Who's there?"

The line went dead.

Tom found the lamp on the floor, switched it on and sat staring at the phone. He looked at his watch. It was 1:30 A.M. Then a loud *brrrrrring* made him jump.

Cautiously lifting the phone, he listened without speaking. Again the breathing, and then a muffled voice.

"Tom Austen?"

"Yes."

"Tom, you must help me. I can give you information, but I'm afraid."

"Who is this?"

"Meet me in the lobby in fifteen minutes, but don't tell anyone. *I beg you.*"

Tom hung up the phone. His hands were trembling. He went to the window and stood looking out at the night. Then he pulled on his clothes, trying to stay calm. He picked up his room key and went into the hallway. Nothing moved, and there was no sound except the low hum of a pop cooler at the end of the corridor.

In the lobby, behind the registration desk, a TV set was playing an old black-and-white movie, but the clerk had fallen asleep. She snorted and groaned in her dreams, then snored quietly. More than fifteen minutes had passed since the call, but no one was waiting for Tom. He checked his watch, then looked at the empty chairs. Lying on one was a sheet of paper. He hurried over, picked it up and read the short message. *Tom Austen: red car in parking lot. Licence number LCC 151. Wait in front seat.*

He was now entering dangerous waters, but the information could be vital, and the person would surely only give it if Tom came alone. For a moment he debated, then approached the desk clerk and shook her arm.

"Huh?" she said, startled. "What is it?"

"I'm sorry to wake you, ma'am. I need your help."

She looked at him through bleary eyes. "What's wrong?"

"I'm going out to the parking lot. If I'm not back in twenty minutes, phone the police."

The woman gave him a strange look. "What are you, crazy? It's two in the morning."

"Licence plate LCC 151. Please remember that for the police." Quickly Tom left the lobby and went into the night. The air was cool, and a dog barked somewhere. Lights along the wall of the motel gave some illumination, but the parking lot seemed a dismal place as he walked slowly around reading licence plates.

At last he found the car, alone in a distant corner of the lot. Tom looked toward the motel, which seemed so far away, then took a deep breath before getting in the front seat. He slammed the door and sat shivering as the minutes passed. Through his mind raced images of the passengers from the *Lady Rose*. Which one was responsible for Vernya's death?

Suddenly two hands covered his face.

Tom yelled in horror. As the hands pressed him fiercely back against the headrest he struggled to free himself. At last he tore loose and turned desperately toward the back seat, fists ready to strike out. Then once again he yelled in shock and surprise.

The person grinning at him from the back seat was his sister, Liz.

"What . . . ? You . . . total fink! How could you do this?"

"It wasn't easy," Liz said, laughing. "It took a while to find an unlocked car."

"But what are you doing here? You're supposed to be in Winnipeg."

"Mom flew out to Victoria for a trial and I came with her. We phoned Ucluelet, because I was going to pay you a surprise visit there, but Mrs. Vangelis said you had been delayed in Port Alberni and were staying in this motel. I took the bus from Victoria and arrived here about 10 P.M." She grinned. "The rest is history."

"You creep! What a way to treat your own brother."

"I know. Wasn't it a riot?"

Laughing, Liz opened her door. As they walked across the parking lot, Tom's mind reeled with a million things he wanted to discuss with his sister. But he waited until they'd passed through the lobby, where the clerk gave him another odd look. In Liz's room he poured out the whole story, right up to the moment when he'd received her mysterious call in the night.

Liz listened carefully and asked a lot of questions, but couldn't figure out a solution to the mystery of Vernya's death.

The next day, after meeting Bunni and Nikki, Liz was sitting in the motel lobby with Tom, watching people walk by, when she did a double take.

"Who is that man in the silk suit?" she whispered, glancing toward the person talking to the desk clerk.

"He's gorgeous. I wish he was a suspect in this case."

Tom smiled. "Your wish is granted. That's Major Tosca."

"*What!* I can't believe my luck." She dug her elbow into Tom's side. "Well, come on, get busy and introduce me."

Tom rolled his eyes, then dragged himself off the sofa and crossed the lobby. A few minutes later he returned with Major Tosca, who was dressed in a black suit and a black tie. Although the man seemed weary, he smiled graciously as Liz was introduced.

"Major Tosca, I'm terribly sorry about your wife."

"Thank you for saying so, Liz. Her death is a terrible blow to me."

"I wish I'd met her. My brother says she was really nice."

Major Tosca smiled at Tom.

"Major, we're thinking of going out for a hamburger. Would you like to come with us?"

"Actually, I would. I haven't been feeling much like eating lately, but I could use a bite of something."

Soon after, they were seated at a corner table in McDonald's, enjoying milkshakes and Big Macs. Major Tosca ate only a small amount, then lit a cigarette and stared out the window. "I notice you used your left hand to light your cigarette," Liz said. "Did you know Leonardo da Vinci painted the Mona Lisa with his left hand?"

Major Tosca smiled. "That sounds like a Trivial Pursuit question. You're probably a champion player."

"I love that game."

"I tell you," Tom said, "if they had a Trivial Pursuit

for superstitious people, Liz would clean up. She knows them all."

For a moment Major Tosca gazed at Liz, then he stood up. "I think I'll get another coffee."

Liz watched him walk toward the counter, then turned to Tom. "He's a nice man, but a prime suspect nonetheless."

"You think he shot his own wife? I doubt it. I watched them together, and they were really in love."

"Stranger things have happened."

"I say Axe did it. That's why he escaped from the *Lady Rose*."

"He's too obvious a suspect. There's more to this case than a guy bumping off his boss because she fired him. We're looking for someone more subtle." Liz finished her milkshake and leaned back with a gentle burp. Then her eyes narrowed. "Don't look now, but there's something going on at the counter."

Across the restaurant, Tom saw Nikki talking to Major Tosca. Dark shadows marked her eyes, and her body seemed to sag as she spoke. Then, suddenly, she burst into tears. Major Tosca reached out sympathetically, but she shook off his hand and quickly left the restaurant.

"Very interesting," Liz said quietly. "Tell me again what Nikki was like on the *Lady Rose*."

"At first, really tense. I remember she fought with Vernya about clear-cut logging. Then, during the storm, she was great. She really took charge in the cabin when people panicked."

"When Vernya was shot, the cabin was dark. Did you say Nikki claimed to be somewhere else, looking for candles?"

"That's right."

"Then, after Vernya's death, she seemed really upset?"

"Yes. I was surprised, because she'd always hated Vernya, but I still felt sorry for her."

"Could it have been an act?"

Tom shrugged. "I don't know."

Liz looked out the window, thinking. When Major Tosca returned with his coffee, she smiled at him. "Did you grow up in Ukee?"

"Yes."

"Did you got to school with Nikki?"

He nodded. "We graduated in the same year."

"Was she in the Drama Club, by any chance?"

"Yes, as a matter of fact." He looked at Liz with interest. "Strange you should ask. Nikki and Vernya appeared together in *Cabaret* during their senior year. Nikki was excellent, and there was talk she would act professionally."

"But she didn't?"

Major Tosca shook his head. "Nikki got married." He lit another cigarette and looked at Liz. "I remember people said it was a mistake for her to marry so young, but Nikki's a very determined person."

"What Nikki wants, Nikki gets?"

"I suppose so." The Major looked closely at Liz. "But that makes her sound tough. She's not really, you know. Nikki is a gentle soul."

"But also passionate?"

The Major nodded. "Yes. She'll really fight for a cause she believes in. Vernya was furious when Nikki worked so hard to get the sewage-dumping law passed. It prevented her from selling the school buildings."

"It's a shame the school was closed down. Was it because of that girl who committed suicide?"

Major Tosca looked out the window. "People in Ukee don't talk about the accident. But since you know that much, I might as well tell the rest. The girl's father, Joseph Larson, blamed Vernya for the girl's death. He started rumours about mismanagement and incompetence. They were all lies, but the other parents believed them." Major Tosca shook his head angrily. "It was a terrible thing to do. It broke Vernya's heart, because she loved the school and her girls. But the parents took them away, and nobody else would attend. Eventually Vernya was forced to shut it down."

"How sad."

"You're right, Liz. It *was* a sad thing, and Vernya was never the same afterwards. I tried to make her forget the whole thing by arranging trips and buying a new home, but nothing has really worked."

"She loved her island," Tom said. "That must have given her some pleasure. It seemed strange she would log it."

"We need the money. Trips to Rome and London are expensive."

As they left McDonald's and began the short walk to the motel, Tom saw Mac watching them from across the street. The man stared intently at Major Tosca until they reached the end of the block and turned a corner.

Tom grabbed Liz's arm. He waited until the Major had walked on, then turned to her. "I just thought of something. Anyone with a grudge against Vernya could also have a grudge against the Major. *What if his life is in danger, too?*"

* * *

For the next few days, Tom kept a close eye on Major Tosca, fearing for his safety. Then the group was given permission by the RCMP to leave Port Alberni, and Tom was no longer able to keep track of the Major's movements. Back in Ucluelet he borrowed a bicycle and rode to the Toscas' house, but there was no sign of life there.

"What should I do?" Tom asked Liz, when he returned to the Vangelis house. "Tell the police?"

She shook her head. "You're getting hysterical. Worrying about the Major isn't going to help us figure out who killed Vernya. Besides, I have a feeling he can look after himself."

"Do you think he's gone into hiding?"

Liz shrugged. "Maybe." She handed him a piece of paper. "By the way, this woman phoned. She's coming at noon to interview you."

"Wow! Do you think she's from the newspaper?" Tom grinned. "Fame at last! Hey, don't look so jealous. Maybe I'll get her to mention your name. There'll be a P.S. to the story: Tom Austen is assisted by his sister, Liz."

"Spare me the honour."

After spending a long time combing his hair for photographs, Tom waited impatiently for the woman's arrival. But then his dreams of glory were dashed.

"You're from an insurance company?" he said in dismay. "You don't want to take my picture?"

"No," the woman said, smiling. "I just want to ask you a few questions about the shooting of Vernya Anastasia Tosca. Her life was insured by my company for a lot of money. Normally we wouldn't pay it until her body is found, but that may never happen. So we're going by your evidence."

"There's no doubt she died. I saw her shot. Then she fell into the ocean. She didn't have a chance."

The woman took out a notebook and asked Tom a number of questions. Finally she smiled at him. "You're an observant person, Tom. I'm impressed. Based on your evidence, I'm sure Major Tosca will be able to collect."

After the woman had left, Liz rushed in demanding a full report on the interview. "Don't say I-told-you-so," she said when Tom had finished. "But if Major Tosca is going to get all that money, he really is a target."

Tom nodded. "What should we do?"

She thought for a minute. "Let's talk to the key suspects and try to find out if they knew about the life insurance."

"It's too bad Axe has disappeared, but we can try Mac. Maybe he'll invite us for tea."

"There's also Nikki," Liz said as a door slammed. "And I think she just came home."

"I wonder where she's been this morning?"

"Good question."

When Nikki came in to say hello, they did their best to learn about her morning activities but got nowhere. She seemed very tired. "I feel so awful about Vernya."

"But you disliked her," Tom said.

"I know, but so what if we fought? That's not important now." Tears appeared in her eyes.

Liz passed Nikki a box of Kleenex. While the woman recovered herself, she watched her carefully. "I hear you were an excellent actress. Didn't you star in *Cabaret*?"

"That's right. I was in it with Vernya."

"That must have been fantastic. I'd love to be in a real play some time. Have you got any souvenirs? Old programs, or maybe some newspaper reviews?"

"I've still got my scrapbook from those days." Nikki stood up, brushing away her tears. Soon she returned with a thick scrapbook and found a page of *Cabaret* souvenirs. A newspaper picture of the cast showed both a glamorous Nikki and a young Vernya with a huge mop of curly hair. Nikki smiled affectionately at the picture. "We were good friends in those days." As she reached for a Kleenex, Liz turned to another page in the scrapbook.

"Hey," she said. "Here's an invitation from your wedding, Nikki." Then she suddenly leaned forward, staring. "The groom was Warwick Tosca. *You were married to the Major!*"

Nikki snatched away the scrapbook. "You're too nosy, Liz. My scrapbook is private."

"I'm sorry. I just . . ."

"Sure I married Warwick Tosca. Then I put him through business school, working in a drugstore to pay our bills." Suddenly she slammed the scrapbook down on a table. "What thanks did I get? *None!* Then Vernya's parents died and he went running to her. Is it any wonder I hated her?"

"I only . . ."

"Leave me alone, Liz. You and Tom get out of here, and stop asking so many questions!" Turning her face, Nikki began to sob, but there was nothing they could do. Quietly Tom followed Liz out of the room and closed the door.

"Let's go to Mac's," he whispered.

"Okay."

Walking toward the harbour they were silent. Then Liz snapped her fingers. "What about the life insurance? We didn't find out if Nikki knew about it."

"I doubt it. Nikki didn't kill Vernya."

"I'm not so sure. Any actress can produce tears on demand."

As they approached Mac's house, the door opened and two people came out. One was a young man with extremely short hair, and the second was a woman. Crossing the footbridge, they looked closely at Tom and Liz, before climbing the hill.

"Who are they?" Liz asked.

Tom shrugged. "Maybe Mac can tell us."

Mac was smiling as he opened the door. The black Lab greeted Tom and Liz eagerly, then stood close to Mac as he prepared tea. The man seemed friendly today. He invited them to enjoy the sunshine on the deck and was pleased when Liz exclaimed over his homemade bread. "It's a treat to have guests from Winnipeg. That's my home town."

"Who were your other guests?" Tom asked.

"That man and woman? They're RCMP investigators."

"Wow! Were they questioning you about Vernya's death?"

Mac shook his head. "These two are on a special team, working with the American FBI. Something to do with counterfeit lottery tickets."

"There was a story on TV about that. What did they want?"

Mac shrugged. "They didn't say. They just asked a lot of questions about people I've worked for locally."

"Maybe they suspect Axe," Tom said. "He used to be a printer. Didn't he work in Major Tosca's print shop once?"

Mac smiled at Liz. "Your brother asks a lot of questions. At least you're better behaved."

Liz laughed. "But I was just going to ask you something, too." She leaned forward. "Did you know that Vernya's life was insured for a lot of money?"

Mac bent down to rub Hogan's head. When he straightened up, he was no longer smiling. "Around here it's bad manners to ask a question like that."

Liz blushed. "I'm sorry."

"It doesn't matter. Now, if you two don't mind I have some things to do."

Quickly Tom and Liz drained their tea, then left the house. The moment they had crossed the footbridge, Liz turned to Tom. "That was interesting!"

"I'll say. Do you think he's hiding something?"

"I'd love to find out." Liz studied the house. "Maybe we should keep an eye on him. If he goes somewhere, we could follow him."

Tom pointed along the waterfront at a tiny wooden building. Above its door faded letters read *Café*. "Let's watch from the window there. Then we can also get a bite to eat."

Liz sighed. "Always thinking of your stomach."

Inside the cafe they found Bunni sitting at the window table with a teenage boy. Smiling, she waved them over. "This is my friend, Andrew Dunning. He was just about to leave for work but come and say hello."

"What do you do?" Tom asked.

"I just graduated from high school," Andrew replied, "and I got lucky. I landed a job as skipper on a cruiser running out from the *Canadian Princess*."

"Hey! You mean those boats that take people whale-watching?"

"That's right. We don't see whales every trip, but it's still a great experience. Why don't you come along? We leave in thirty minutes."

Tom hesitated. He'd been dying to go whale-watching since arriving in Ucluelet, but there was the investigation to consider. He looked out the window at Mac's house, wondering what to do. "Say, Liz, could you shadow him alone?"

"I'm not sure," Liz answered. She was staring at Andrew with an expression Tom had seen before. "Am I invited whale-watching, too?" she asked.

Andrew smiled. "Of course."

She turned to Tom and winked. "We can always shadow Mac tomorrow."

9

The cruiser was white, with sleek lines. "Welcome to the *Nootka Princess*," Andrew said as they approached along a dock. "Once we're at sea, come to the wheelhouse for a visit."

A number of tourists were crowded into the enclosed cabin, but Tom and Liz found seats in the stern. Then they noticed a narrow deck forward, and went to stand there. Leaning against the cabin, they turned their faces to the sun.

The cruiser's twin engines rumbled into life and diesel fumes filled the air. Slipping away from the dock, the *Nootka Princess* moved slowly out of the harbour past the many fishing boats at their wharves. "What a great view," Liz said. "I think I'll stay in Ukee forever."

Tom laughed. "Because of Andrew Dunning?"

"You've got to admit, he's very handsome in that captain's cap."

"Not to mention that sun-bleached hair. He's almost as blond as Bunni."

"Bunni is okay, but I'm glad she didn't come with us. Those sunglasses of hers are a bit much."

"Picky, picky, picky. You just wish you were born blond."

With a sudden surge of power the cruiser leapt ahead through the sea. Enormous waves rolled away from the hull and spray whipped back from the bow, lashing their faces. Looking toward the stern, Tom saw that the water was a foaming mass of white and green, churned up by the propellers that drove the boat rapidly out into the open ocean.

A door opened forward, and Andrew leaned out. "Come on in!" he called. "I'm getting lonely."

"Here I go." Liz grinned at Tom. "Why don't you stay out here, little brother, and enjoy the view?"

"No way." Tom followed Liz forward, leaning into the wind. "I think I should come along and tell Andrew you eat peanut butter with your fingers."

"Don't you dare!"

They found Andrew sitting on a tall padded chair, one hand gripping the stainless-steel wheel and the other on the twin levers that controlled the power. A large floating compass was in front of him, plus a radio, depth sounder and radar.

"You could go all the way to China in this thing," Tom said. "You've got everything."

Andrew smiled. "It's a nice life. I come from a sea-faring family, so I've been in boats since I was little.

This job also gives me a chance to see lots of birds. That's my real hobby."

"I bet you're the guy who took Bunni to see the cormorant nests at Long Beach."

"Ke-rect."

Liz smiled at Andrew. "I wouldn't mind seeing those nests."

"How about tomorrow? It's my day off."

"Wonderful."

Deciding he wasn't needed in the wheelhouse, Tom went out on deck. Licking his salty lips, he held tight to the railing as the *Nootka Princess* smashed through the sea toward a rocky islet. It was pounded by waves that gushed straight up as they hit the rocks, throwing white water everywhere. At the top of the islet were large brown shapes that Tom thought were logs until one raised its head.

"Sea lions! I don't believe it!"

The other tourists rushed to the railing with their cameras as the *Nootka Princess* cut its speed. They glimpsed a sea lion swimming through the green water which foamed around the islet, then aimed their lenses at a great blubbery animal sprawled on top of the rocks as it lifted a sleek head to snuffle the wind.

Liz joined Tom at the railing. "I forgot to bring my camera."

"Me, too, and nobody at school's going to believe we saw this."

"Andrew says our next stop is at Nearby Island, to see the bald eagles." Liz gazed at the island as they approached. A band of cloud ringed its summit, and the rainforest was a thick blanket of solid green between sea and sky. The cruiser slipped past a sandy beach and then came to a stop in the shelter of a high cliff. Andrew dropped a fishing line into the water and almost immediately pulled up a sea bass. When it was dead he threw the fish high into the air. As it landed on the sea with a loud *splat*, the cruiser powered away a short distance, then stopped.

"Here they come!" Andrew called, pointing toward the top of the cliff. "Get those cameras ready."

Two eagles appeared from a large nest high in the trees. Soaring on magnificent wings, they swept out over the water. Swooping and dipping, the eagles circled lower and lower until one dropped straight down to the surface. Then it rose again into the air with the sea bass in its talons, and flew back to the nest with its mate.

The tourists burst into applause.

"Honest, folks, we don't pay the eagles to do that stunt," Andrew grinned. "But I guess they know that a cruiser stopping here means a free meal. Now we'll head for Captain Cook Cove to have some refreshments ourselves."

As the cruiser started forward again, Andrew invited Tom and Liz back inside. "A penguin has been spotted near here, and a leatherback turtle got tangled in a fishing boat's nets. Can you imagine a penguin or a six-hundred-kilogram tropical turtle in these waters?" He pointed out the window at a bird with a long neck, swimming nearby.

"That's a common murre. They feed on candlefish and needlefish. Sometimes they get so full they can't take off. They just race along the surface, madly flapping their wings."

"What about the whales?" Tom asked. "Aren't we going to see any?"

Andrew shook his head. "It doesn't look like it. Some days they're just not around."

A few minutes later the cruiser dropped anchor in a sheltered cove of Nearby Island. Andrew lowered a small motorboat at the stern and ferried tourists ashore. It took several trips, with Tom and Liz the last to make the short journey. "Is this safe?" Liz asked. "Aren't you afraid of that old hermit? What was his name again? He almost attacked Tom once. He sounds crazy."

Andrew shook his head. "Mosquito Joe is dead."

"How do you know?"

"Didn't you hear? They came across his shack on the island, just before they had to stop logging. The shack was deserted. And an overturned canoe was found washed up in this very cove. People say he drowned accidentally . . . or committed suicide."

"But the canoe could have belonged to anyone!"

"Maybe so, but most people think he's dead. At last he's at peace. His spirit can roam the rainforest beside his daughter."

"What do you mean?"

"I thought you knew. She's the girl who committed suicide at the school. In those days his name was Joseph Larson. After he got the school shut down, he started living on the island. He became a hermit. People figure all he wanted was to be near his daughter's spirit."

"Wow," Liz said, shivering. "That is really creepy." As they reached the beach, she looked up at the massive trees of the rainforest. "What a spectacular place. I'd love to explore a bit."

Andrew checked his watch. "Want to spend a few hours here? I have to take these tourists home to Ukee, then come back this evening with some more people. I could pick you up in this cove at 2100 hours."

Liz looked at her brother. "What do you think?"

"What about Mosquito Joe's spirit? And his daughter?"

Liz glanced at Andrew, then smiled bravely. "That doesn't bother me."

Andrew nodded. "Okay, but don't be late meeting me. Otherwise you'll have to camp on the beach overnight and get picked up in the morning. You might find it chilly."

"Don't worry, we'll be here at 2100 hours."

After refreshments on the beach with the others, Tom and Liz stood by the forest watching the cruiser leave. They waved until it was out of sight, then turned to push a path into the thick undergrowth. The forest closed around them.

"Look at all the shades of green!" Tom said. Where the trees were shadowed, their mossy trunks were a black-green, while the needles on their branches were a brighter colour. The ferns covering the ground were a vivid green, as was the moss lit by the thin shafts of sunshine slipping down among the trees.

"That tree bending over the stream looks like it's made of green velvet," Liz said. "Look at all the moss on it. No wonder this is called rainforest."

They walked to the edge of the stream to gaze at the water bubbling among the rocks. It looked black and cold, except where slanting sunshine lit the golden rocks on the bed of the stream.

"Think we can cross the water on those boulders?"

"Nope," Liz answered. "They look too slippery."

"Where's your sense of adventure?" Tom jumped to the first boulder, then went quickly to another. For a moment he wobbled there, feeling the water leap up to splash his legs, then jumped to a larger boulder. His feet skidded on the wet moss and he quickly went to another perch. He was beginning to regret his decision, but it was too late now to turn back. Trying not to think how cold the water would be, he took several more boulders with long jumps and finally hopped ashore to raise triumphant arms. "I did it!" he shouted. Turning to gloat at his sister, he saw her reach the last boulder and jump effortlessly to his side.

"Nothing to it," she said, grinning.

A few minutes later they entered a clearing and saw a bird clinging to the side of a tree. Sunshine glinted from its long bill, and its red head was tilted back as though listening for sounds. But it didn't seem bothered by Tom and Liz as they crept closer to watch.

"Do you think it's a woodpecker?" Liz whispered.

"Probably."

The bird put its bill into a small hole in the tree trunk, then leaned back to swallow. When Tom and Liz got too close, the bird flew away. Going forward to investigate, they discovered a number of holes neatly drilled into the trunk.

"They're full of water. That must be how it drinks."

Tom sighed. "If this island became a park, anyone could see that bird in the wild. That's what the natives want, and I think it's a great idea."

"Do any natives live on the island now?"

Tom shook his head. "Nikki says they were kicked off generations ago. Nobody paid them for their island, so now they want it back. They want to stop it being logged."

Liz looked up at the trees. "Now I can understand why Greenpeace is helping the natives. This is such a beautiful place."

Dead branches snapped underfoot as they continued through the forest, smelling the sweet air. In another clearing they discovered a pond surrounded by trees. Sunlight flooded down, silhouetting the black trees and giving them a fuzzy green outline where the moss on their trunks was lit by sunshine.

"Yike!" Liz grabbed Tom's arm. "Look at that spider!"

Close by, shining in the rays of the sun, was a large web. At its centre was a hairy black spider. As it scuttled down the web, Tom shook his head. "You scared it, Liz. The poor little thing."

"The poor *huge* thing! We could have walked straight into it."

"So what?"

Liz rolled her eyes. "A spider in the morning, beware its warning."

"That's a great superstition," Tom said, glancing at his watch, "but it's no longer morning."

"If a spider crawls down, some poor soul may drown." Shivering, Liz looked around the forest. "We shouldn't have come here. That girl's spirit may be watching us."

"Not to mention the ghost of Mosquito Joe." Lifting his eyes, Tom stared at the forest just behind Liz. "Maybe we should head back to the cove."

"Good idea. Which way is it?"

Tom looked at the forest. Suddenly it resembled a green wall, with absolutely no doors. "Um . . . I think our path is just over . . . past those cedars. Or maybe. . ."

"Haven't you been keeping track of our route?"

Tom shook his head. "I thought you were. But don't worry. I'll find it." He led the way into the forest, but the path they'd followed for so long had disappeared.

He pushed aside some bushes, hoping to find the path, then looked at the trees which rose high above. They all looked the same. There was no familiar landmark to guide them back to the cove.

"There!" he exclaimed. "It's the woodpecker, back on its tree again. Now I know where we are."

"Maybe it's a different tree. Or a different bird."

"You're right." Tom sighed deeply. "Liz, I'm getting worried. I think we're lost."

"We could find that stream and follow it to the ocean. Then maybe we'd be able to spot the cove."

"Good thinking."

Once again they plunged through the forest.

For a while Tom felt optimistic, but his hopes began to fade as time passed. Sunlight no longer slanted down through the trees, and the forest was suddenly much darker. Straight ahead, water seemed to be gushing from high in the trees.

"Am I going crazy?" he said. "What is that?"

"A waterfall, I think."

Pushing closer through the undergrowth, they saw a steep hill. Water plunged down its side, hidden in some places by the trees, then suddenly leaping into view as it fell toward the forest floor.

"I've got an idea." Tom pointed at the hill. "There might be a view from the top. Maybe we'll be able to see the cove from there."

The climb was very difficult. Often they had to use exposed roots to pull themselves up the hill, and their legs ached with the strain. But finally the hill levelled off and they stumbled into a clearing. It contained rocks and wild grass and a few thin trees, but they were able to see the ocean without difficulty.

As they hurried forward, Liz held out a warning hand. "That's a cliff ahead. Don't get too close."

From the cliff edge they looked out to sea. The water was golden, lit by the sun as it sank toward the horizon. They saw the black outline of a tug towing a raft of logs in the distance and, in a cove along the shore, the sleek lines of Andrew's cruiser.

"He's here already!" Liz exclaimed. "What's the time?"

"2045. It took longer to climb the hill than we thought."

"We'll never reach the cove in fifteen minutes! We're going to be left behind."

"Let's try yelling."

Waving their arms, jumping up and down, they screamed until they were hoarse. But it was hopeless. "The cruiser's too far away," Tom said. "Get a mirror out of your purse, and flash sunlight their way. That always works in the movies."

"You must be joking. Why would I be carrying a purse?" Liz sat down on a rock to stare at the cruiser. "I don't believe this is happening."

"Maybe Andrew is looking for us with his binoculars."

"Then why has he started the engines?" Liz pointed at the white wake that had suddenly churned up behind the cruiser. "And why is he going away?"

Tom watched the cruiser move out of the cove, then checked his watch. "2100 hours on the nose. He's very efficient."

"I may never see him again, Tom. It's all your fault."

"We may never see anyone again, unless we figure out what to do."

"Andrew said to sleep on the beach overnight."

"I'm not crazy about that."

"Neither am I. What about that girl's ghost? It might come around."

Tom kicked a stone over the cliff edge, then walked slowly away from Liz, thinking. Finally he reached the distant end of the cliff. Below him the island was covered entirely by the forest except in one place where a number of buildings stood in a clearing.

"The school! That's where we can go."

10

Shortly after, they reached the bottom of the hill. Scratched by a hundred bushes and drenched in sweat, they were tired and hungry. "I'm not crazy about your idea," Liz said. "That school sounds creepy."

"It's better than spending the night outdoors."

"What about that voice you heard?"

Tom managed a smile. "Maybe it was my imagination. Try to relax, Liz. You *know* there are no such things as ghosts."

Liz looked at a nearby beach. "Are you positive this is the right direction?"

"Trust me. We'll just follow the beach to that point of land and find the school on the other side. I figured out the route from up on the cliff."

The sand was soft under their feet. Big waves rolled

in to thump against the beach as they trudged wearily along, watching the seagulls soaring above. "The wind's picking up," Liz said. "Maybe another storm's coming."

But Tom wasn't listening. He was looking toward the forest. The trees seemed to be on fire in the light of the dying sun. "Hey! I just saw something!"

"Quit trying to freak me."

"Honest, Liz, I just saw a shape among the trees." Running into the forest, he pointed toward a clump of trees. The twisted, moss-covered branches were like tangled green hair. The branches trembled, then something slipped away into the darkness of the rainforest. "That was Mosquito Joe!" Tom exclaimed.

"Or his spirit," Liz said. "Let's get out of here."

They returned quickly to the beach. As they hurried toward the point neither spoke, but both glanced frequently over their shoulders. The sun plunged into the sea, and darkness began to creep across the island.

"I wish you hadn't seen that ghost, or whatever it was," Liz said as they reached the point and paused for breath. She looked across the ocean at the sweeping beam of a lighthouse. The rich colour of the orange sky was reflected on the sea, where seagulls swam among the black lines of floating kelp.

Then a cry sounded from the forest.

"What was that?"

"Probably just the Lord of the Night."

"The what?"

"It was an owl, Liz. Nothing to worry about."

"*An owl!*" Liz stared at the forest, wide-eyed. "If

you hear the owl call your name, it's a warning of approaching death."

"Maybe so, but it didn't cry Liz, Liz. Or did it? *Liz, Liz, in your future doom is.*"

"Quit joking, Tom. I'm really scared."

"Then let's keep moving. I'm sure we're close to the school." Crossing his fingers, Tom moved on with Liz close behind. It was a relief when the trees thinned out and he saw the outline of several buildings, their white walls standing out against the murky darkness.

"The school! We did it."

"Well, at least it's better than being in the forest."

"Look at the chess board." Tom crossed the tall grass of an abandoned lawn to look at the giant board set into the ground between two benches. A garden swing was nearby, its canvas rotting away, and a rose bush grew wild beside it. Liz sniffed one of the yellow blooms.

"How sad to think of the girls who used to come here. I wonder where they are now?"

"One may roam the rainforest."

"Cut that out." Liz looked at a wooden structure beside the ocean. "That looks like a boathouse. Maybe there's an abandoned boat we could use."

"I don't think it would be a good idea to . . ."

And then, suddenly, they heard the voice. "*Beware,*" it cried. "*Beware! Beware!*"

Screaming, Liz ran for the forest. Tom also raced for the shelter of the trees. Then a bell began to clang. As the terrible sound rang out, and the watery voice continued to cry *beware*, Tom and Liz crashed through the dark forest. Then Tom tripped and fell to his knees. As Liz helped him up, Tom stared at her.

"Wait a minute! That bell doesn't make sense."

"What do you mean?"

"When I looked at the old photograph of the resort, I saw a building with a bell tower. I'm sure that's a real bell, Liz. Since when do ghosts ring real bells?" He looked in the direction of the school. "I'm going to take a look. Are you coming with me?"

Shivering, Liz hugged her body. "I don't have any choice. I'm not staying here alone."

They crept forward through the trees. Over and over the watery voice cried *beware*, but Tom smiled grimly and kept going. Again they reached the abandoned school. Tom pointed at a building that stood at the top of the slope. "There's the tower. Let's go see what's making the bell ring."

"I'm sure it's that ghost. She's warning us to stay away." Liz covered her ears. "This is horrible, Tom."

"Come on!" Waving at Liz, he ran toward the building with the bell tower. The night was now so dark that he kept stumbling, but soon they reached the building. Paint had peeled off in huge flakes, leaving behind rotting black wood.

"I remember this was the resort's dance hall, but it looks like Vernya used it as a gym. Do you see the old basketball hoop lying near the door?" Tiptoeing across the porch, his mouth dry, Tom opened the door.

"It's completely dark," Liz whispered. "I can't see a thing."

They stepped inside. The clanging of the bell filled the black air and made goosebumps rise on Tom's skin. The air smelled of old, wet wood. As he stepped forward his foot hit a ball and it bounced away, making a hollow echo in the darkness.

The dreadful *clang-clang, clang-clang* continued as they moved forward. Something brushed against Tom's face, making his heart jump. Then he realized it was a climbing rope which hung from a beam above. "Isn't that a sliver of light straight ahead? I think it's coming from under a door."

"You're right."

As the bell tolled, they moved across the gym to the door and opened it. Light spilled into their eyes. For a moment Tom could only blink. Then he saw a spiral staircase. Together with Liz he climbed the winding stairs until they reached a wide platform. Standing on it, pulling hard on the bell rope, was Vernya Anastasia Tosca.

* * *

"I don't believe it!" Tom gasped.

Liz turned to run, but stopped when Vernya dropped the rope and pulled a small gun from her pocket. Smiling, she motioned Liz to Tom's side.

"I don't believe it!" he said.

Vernya chuckled. "You're repeating yourself." She looked at Liz. "I know this boy, but who are you?"

"I'm Tom's sister, Liz. Are you a ghost?"

"I'm as real as this gun." Vernya picked up a flashlight from the floor and waved them toward the stairs. "Down you go. I'll be right behind, so no monkey business."

"What's going to happen to us?"

"I haven't decided, but a couple of meddling kids aren't going to spoil things now."

"I can't believe you're alive!" Tom exclaimed. "But why were you ringing the bell?"

"Enough questions! Any more, and I'll gag you both."

They followed the flashlight beam across the gym. Tom was tempted to make a break for safety, but was too afraid that Vernya would use the gun. His mind reeled. Nothing made sense.

Outside the gym, the watery voice continued to cry *beware!* Somewhere in the forest a night creature produced a single loud cry, then fell silent. "This way," Vernya said, leading them to a small wooden building. As she removed a padlock and opened the door, the smell of chemicals came to them.

"This was the school's chem lab," Vernya said, flicking on a light. At the front of the lab were old wooden desks. Beyond them stood rows of high counters containing test tubes and beakers.

"Look at all the chemicals," Liz said, pointing at shelves of big bottles. "This place would blow sky-high in a fire."

Red lights glowed from something that looked like a large radio. Vernya flipped a switch on it and immediately the ghostly voice was silent.

"So!" Tom exclaimed. "The ghost was a fake."

Vernya smiled. "It's a nice way to keep people away from here. All around the school grounds are photo-electric cells sending out invisible beams of light. The moment a person steps through a beam, this machine is triggered. It starts broadcasting the ghostly voice from hidden speakers."

"But why keep people away? What's going on here?"

"That's none of your business, young man."

Liz looked at Vernya. "Did one of your students really commit suicide?"

The woman nodded, looking sad. "She was an unhappy little creature, and so lonely. I did everything possible to make her feel better, but it didn't work. Finally I wrote to her father in Calgary and suggested she be taken home. But he'd just gone through a divorce and didn't feel ready to look after his little girl yet." She sighed. "I think it was the last straw, feeling rejected by her dad. Shortly after, the tragedy happened."

"People say her father blamed the school."

"He was devastated, and probably felt guilty. Whatever the reason, he decided to get revenge. It worked, too. I lost the school. It was my entire life . . ." Vernya's voice trailed off.

"Please let us go, Vernya."

"Not a chance." She sighed, then motioned with the gun. "Get outside, and make it fast."

A weed-choked path led to another small building. "You're going into storage," Vernya said, opening the door. "Don't think you can escape. I'll be back soon."

The door closed. Then they heard the rattle of metal as it was locked. Tom looked around for a means of escape, but there were no windows. The walls were painted purple and covered with a few peeling travel posters. The tiny room also contained a small carpet, one soggy armchair and a rusty stove.

"This must have been a meeting room for the kids."

"What should we do?"

"We've got to do something. I don't like the way Vernya keeps waving that gun around." Tom pointed at a trap door in the floor. "I didn't notice that before. Maybe it leads to a tunnel!" Quickly he removed a lock from the trap door and pulled it open, but found only a small space that had probably been used to store boxes. "We can't hide there. Vernya would find us in two seconds." As he began to close the door, Liz grabbed his arm.

"Don't shut that! I've got a plan." Dragging the small carpet across the room, she covered the hole in the floor. Then she lay down near the carpet. "Turn out the light and hide against the wall, Tom. When Vernya comes in, be ready to slam the trap door closed."

As Tom waited in the darkness, his heart thudded in his chest. If Liz's plan didn't work, there was no telling what Vernya would do. Then he heard footsteps crossing the porch, and the rattle of the lock. Taking a deep breath, he watched the door slowly open. As a dark figure stepped into the room, Liz began to moan. "My stomach," she cried, rolling back and forth on the floor. "Oh, I'm sick."

The figure hurried across the carpet toward her. Then, with a terrible cry, the dark shape crashed through the opening to the space below. Leaping forward, Tom slammed the trap door closed. Quickly he locked it.

"That worked beautifully, but there's one problem!"

"What's that?" Liz asked.

"The person we just trapped wasn't Vernya."

"Then who was it?"

"Axe!" Tom stared at his sister. "We'd better get out of here, and fast."

11

Tom and Liz dashed outside. "We've got to hide! Vernya can't be far away. Let's try that big building down the hill."

Racing to it, they found an unlocked door and hurried inside. In the dim light they saw a long hallway with doors opening off both sides. The smell of chalk was thick in the air. "It's a classroom block. There's got to be someplace to hide here."

But the first room they entered was empty. A few textbooks were stacked in a corner, and an old coat hung from a hook, but there was no furniture to hide behind. Moving along the hallway, they tried another classroom, but it was also empty.

Opening yet another door, Tom gasped in surprise. The classroom contained heavy machinery. "Those look like printing presses. What are they . . .?"

Suddenly Liz gripped Tom's arm. "She's coming! I can see a flashlight outside!"

"Should we hide in here?"

"No! These presses must be what Vernya's protecting, so we can't be caught near them."

"How about that room at the end of the hall?" Rushing to the door, Tom yanked it open and they stumbled inside. He dropped to his knees and crawled through the blackness until he reached a wall. Feeling his way forward, he touched the rough fabric of a sofa.

"Over here, Liz!" he whispered. "We can hide behind this."

The dim shape of his sister came out of the darkness. They pushed the sofa away from the wall, then crawled behind it and lay listening to the darkness. Feet came along the hall. Then the door opened.

"I know they're somewhere close by," Vernya muttered. "They haven't had time to get out of the school."

The flashlight beam flicked around the room. Tom held his breath as it touched the wall beside the sofa before moving on. Dust tickled his nostrils, and for a moment he was desperately afraid that he would sneeze. Finally the door closed, and he was able to rub his nose. For a long time there was silence. Through the window they could see the beam of light from Vernya's flashlight as she explored the grounds. Then Liz leaned close to Tom's ear.

"Now what?"

"We can't stay here. She's bound to come back. Come on. There's another floor upstairs."

Opening the door, they went into the hallway. "We'd better hurry," Tom said, starting forward into the black air. "Do you know where the stairs are?"

When Liz didn't reply, Tom's skin prickled with fear. Somehow he knew that things had gone terribly wrong. Turning, he saw the pale shape of Liz in the darkness. Gripping her was Major Tosca.

Minutes later they were again facing Vernya. She had been summoned back inside by Major Tosca, and she looked angry. "You troublemakers! How did you escape?"

"My plan was simple," Tom said, "and it worked perfectly."

Liz stared at him. "*Your* plan?"

"Well . . ." He turned to Vernya. "Anyway, maybe you've caught us again, but at least we trapped Axe."

"Axe!" Vernya stared at the Major. "I suspected he might be on the island, watching us. Didn't I warn you?"

Major Tosca nodded. "You were right, but now he seems to be no longer a threat, thanks to our young friends."

"But," Tom said, "you mean Axe was trying to help *us*?"

Vernya laughed. "That's right. You're too clever for your own good." Then she frowned. "What are you two doing on this island in the middle of the night, anyway?"

"We were dropped off by a cruiser from Ukee," Liz said. "It will be back any minute. If Andrew can't find us, the police will come searching."

"Trying to scare us? It won't work." But the woman did look worried as she turned to her husband. "We've got to move fast."

"No problem. I've almost finished loading the launch. I'll be ready soon."

"What about these kids?"

"I've got plans. They won't cause any more trouble."

Tom looked at him. "Please, Major Tosca, let us go."

He shook his head.

"Then at least tell us what's happening at this school."

Major Tosca smiled and led them to the room containing the printing presses. As he switched on lights, Tom noticed the windows had been covered with plywood. "That's to prevent anyone seeing the lights at night," Major Tosca said. "Sometimes a boat passes by. People have occasionally landed to explore, but up until now the voice scared them away. We didn't want anyone to discover these presses."

"What are they for?"

"Making counterfeit lottery tickets." Major Tosca smiled. "It was a great plan! After my printing company in Ukee went out of business, I moved the presses over here. Axe came with me to help make phoney Washington state lottery tickets. We printed many different number combinations, then smuggled the tickets across the border. On my first try I claimed five thousand dollars. When nobody in the lottery office said a word about the phoney ticket, I knew I'd make big money."

"But then you tried to claim first prize, and someone else showed up with the same number. You ran from the office, and the police started looking for you. I saw it all on television."

The Major shook his head, sighing. "It was the worst

possible luck, having that woman arrive at the office with her winning ticket. Unfortunately I left my counterfeit ticket behind when I ran. I understand the police have identified the type of paper and ink used, and have tracked me as far as Ukee. But an hour from now I'll be gone, and they'll never find me."

"Where are you going?"

He smiled. "You'll soon know."

"Did you fire Axe because you're pulling out?"

"That's right. But he made those plates himself, and seemed to think we owed him something."

"Your phoney ghost worked on me that night I came here to investigate. If Mac had been with me we might have actually found the presses. I wouldn't have been scared off so easily."

Major Tosca nodded. "I knew you were planning to visit the school with Mac. Axe followed you to his place earlier and heard you making arrangements to visit the island. That night, Axe and I stole Mac's dog. We told Mac he'd only get the dog back if he disappeared from the house before you arrived. But I never thought you'd have the guts to go to the island on your own."

"Some guts. I was so scared when I heard that voice, I couldn't get off the island fast enough." Tom shook his head. "But what's the bell for? I didn't hear it that night."

"When an intruder tripped the alarm, and the voice started, one of us would usually run to the bell tower to make some extra noise. But we didn't bother when you came in Mac's boat. We saw you run."

"So *you* wrote the note I found at Mac's place. It

was left-handed writing, and you use your cigarette lighter with your left hand."

"Clever boy, but it's a bit late now to play detective."

"Poor Mac. What a lousy thing to do—stealing his dog." Tom snapped his fingers. "But you *didn't* give the dog back! That's why Mac wouldn't answer any of my questions the next day. He was still afraid for Hogan."

"And that's why he was so upset when he found out you were leaving town," Liz said.

The Major smiled. "He got the dog back eventually. I kept my promise."

"Why *was* Mac fired as caretaker? So he wouldn't see the printing presses?"

"That's right. It's too bad about his job, but that's the way it goes."

Liz shook her head. "You use people, Major, and I think that's terrible." She looked at Vernya. "Did he marry you for your money?"

"Of course not."

Liz studied her face. "He was married to Nikki until your parents died. Then you inherited a lot of money and suddenly he was in love with you. It's all beginning to make sense. It was probably the Major's idea to log the island. He wanted the money and didn't care what you wanted."

"That's . . . that's not true," Vernya protested.

"Okay, so you're *both* money-hungry, and I bet that's why Vernya was shot on the *Lady Rose*."

A sudden grin lit Major Tosca's handsome face. "It was a brilliant plan! When the natives got their court injunction and ruined our hopes of logging the island, I had to think of another way to make money. The counterfeit lottery tickets scheme had turned sour, but there was still Vernya's life insurance."

"Which was worth a fortune."

"Yes, but only with her dead." He chuckled. "The simple answer was to fake her death. But of course the insurance company would want proof before they'd pay up. So she needed to die at sea, where her body could be lost forever, and . . ."

"I know," Tom said angrily. "And you needed a witness to tell the police he'd seen Vernya killed. So you played me for a sucker."

Major Tosca laughed. "Actually, I'd expected that one of the crew members would be the witness. But you were great, Tom Austen, and I thank you."

"Who was the person crouching behind the lifeboat? Was it you?"

"Of course. There were blanks in my gun, and Vernya had a capsule in her mouth. She bit it, and fake blood poured out. She spun backwards, pretended to grab at the railing, then went over the side. What an actress!"

"But what happened then?"

Vernya smiled. "A launch was waiting to pick me up. It was driven by a friend of the Major's, who'd come from Seattle just to do the job. He brought me back to the school, where I've been hiding out waiting for the insurance money to be paid."

"Weren't you afraid, falling off the *Lady Rose* in a storm?"

"We hadn't expected bad weather, but we decided to

go ahead with the plan. I have to admit the water was cold."

"Have you noticed," Liz said, "that it's always you doing the hard things? Falling off the *Lady Rose*, logging your island, selling your beautiful house at the Point. He even made you betray Nikki, who used to be your friend."

"Enough talk! There's work to do before we leave." Major Tosca looked at his wife. "I need fifteen minutes to finish loading our things on the launch. In the meantime, you keep an eye on these kids."

Vernya motioned at Tom and Liz with the gun. "Get moving."

Outside, the air smelled of approaching rain. Tom took a deep breath, then looked at the storm clouds rapidly covering the night sky. They had only a short time to escape. Somehow he had to distract Vernya's attention from her gun.

"This is such a magnificent island, Vernya," he said casually. "No wonder you don't want it logged."

Silence.

Liz turned to her. "Major Tosca's using you, Vernya. He doesn't love you."

She smiled. "What do you know about love, Liz? I'm a grown woman. I know what I'm doing."

"He's tricky, Vernya. Be careful."

Tom looked at the other buildings. Something had to happen *soon* or they were finished.

"What's that big building down the hill?"

"The auditorium is in there, and the dining hall. It cost me a fortune to build."

"I bet it's beautiful. Could we see it? Or wouldn't the Major approve?"

"Of course we can see it," Vernya said. "We've got a few minutes."

"Great." As they started walking, Tom looked at Vernya. "I bet the kids liked you."

"I guess that's true. But I was firm with them. Discipline is important."

"Was the food good?"

"The girls didn't like the meatloaf. They called it dead man's leg." She laughed.

"Do you miss them?"

"Very much." Opening the door, Vernya switched on some lights. Windows surrounded them all around the walls of the auditorium. Red velvet chairs faced a large stage, where lighting equipment could be seen. At the back of the stage was a mural showing a whale, a seal and a salmon. "I had an artist make that out of mosaic tiles," Vernya said proudly. "You see how they glitter in the lights?"

"It's beautiful."

"Do you want to see the kitchen? The equipment is excellent."

It was a large area behind the auditorium. Dust and discarded supplies were scattered on tables and shelves. Vernya showed them the huge stoves and dishwashers, drawer after drawer of cutlery, and rotary machines designed to make twenty slices of toast at once. On one wall was a walk-in refrigerator with its enormous door standing open. Through the door they could see the many racks where food had once been stored.

"Isn't this thing dangerous?" Tom asked. "What if the door closed with someone inside?"

"Air comes in through a grill in the wall and, besides . . ."

Tom spotted a lightbulb lying on a table. Suddenly he had a plan.

"Wait a minute!" he whispered. "I heard footsteps!"

"Where?"

"Upstairs. Maybe it's Axe."

Vernya looked up at the ceiling. As she did Tom snatched the lightbulb and threw it with all his energy into the walk-in refrigerator. As it exploded inside with a loud *BLAM!* he dropped to his knees, clutching his stomach.

"I'm shot! I'm shot!"

Vernya stared at him, then looked into the darkness of the refrigerator. Raising the gun, she walked slowly forward. "Who's in there? Is it you, Axe?" Reaching the door, she stepped cautiously inside.

Leaping forward, Liz slammed the door. As Vernya's faint cries sounded from inside the refrigerator, Tom jumped up, grinning. "Good work, kiddo."

"Gimme five," she said, slapping his hand. "That was a brilliant move with the lightbulb."

"We're not safe yet. There's still Major Tosca to worry about." Quickly they ran from the kitchen to the auditorium. "Kill those lights! He could see us from outside." As Liz flicked the switch, plunging the auditorium into darkness, a loud *screech!* sounded from somewhere inside the building.

"What was that!"

"Ssssh," Liz whispered, grabbing Tom's arm. "Hide behind these chairs." Ducking down, they stared into the black air. Creaks and groans sounded from the walls and floors of the building, and then they heard footsteps. Slowly they approached through the darkness, stopped for a moment, and then came closer. Suddenly the lights went on. Unable to contain his curiosity, Tom raised his head. Standing beside the light switch was Vernya.

"You didn't let me finish my sentence about the walk-in," she said, smiling. "Air comes in through a grill in the wall and, besides, there's a safety latch inside. Anyone who gets trapped just pushes the latch and the door opens. I notice, however, that the hinges need oiling."

Once again, Tom and Liz were marched at gunpoint into the night. Vernya led them to an open field, where they met Major Tosca. Wiping sweat from his forehead, he gestured toward the dark shape of the distant boathouse. "The launch is warming up. There's one last job to do, but I need Axe's help." He turned to Tom and Liz. "Where is he?"

"We won't tell."

"I've got news for you. A few minutes from now all these buildings will be on fire. If Axe is trapped inside one, he'll die."

As Tom and Liz stared at him in horror, Vernya gasped. "What are you talking about?"

"I'll tell you soon, sweetheart." He turned to Tom and Liz. "Well? Where is Axe?"

As Tom hesitated, wondering if the man was bluffing, Liz spoke up. "He's in the girls' meeting room. We trapped him in that space under the floor."

"Thank you, Liz." Major Tosca looked at his wife. "Take them to the launch."

"But the fire. What is this all about?"

"Trust me, my darling." Turning, he hurried into the night.

"Vernya!" Liz exclaimed. "You've got to help us. We can all escape in the launch!"

"Be quiet." Vernya motioned with her gun. "Get moving."

Within minutes they had crossed the wild grass and entered the boathouse. Faint light came through a large opening to the ocean. Ropes and paddles hung on the walls, a canoe rested on a small platform, and waves washed around the classic old launch facing the sea.

Brass rails gleamed along the deck, and there was a small lifeboat on the roof of the wheelhouse. Vernya motioned Tom and Liz toward the gangway and they climbed it to the deck. Reaching the wheelhouse, they found more brass inside. It shone on the instrument panel and on the handle of a closed door which seemed to connect to a cabin. From somewhere below decks they heard the low rumble of the engine warming up.

Vernya motioned Tom and Liz toward benches beside a small table. The moment they sat down, Liz began talking. She tried desperately to convince the woman to help them escape in the launch, but Vernya was silent, staring out the window. Then Major Tosca appeared in the doorway with Axe. They struggled inside with a large carton and lowered it to the deck. Major Tosca shoved the carton against the cabin's closed door, then wiped his forehead.

"That's heavy! There are parts of a printing press inside. When I knew Axe could help me carry them, I decided to take one press along." He slapped the huge man on the back. "Axe is back on our team. A good printer is hard to find, and we may need his services again." The Major winked. "He's coming to Oregon with us."

As Axe beamed happily, Liz stared at him. "Don't trust him, Axe! He'll doublecross you again."

"Who are you, kid?"

The Major laughed. "Come on, Axe, we've got some more cartons to load. Then we'll be leaving."

As soon as the men had left, Liz tried again to get Vernya's help. But it was useless, and soon the other cartons had been placed against the door.

"And now, my darling, I have a task for you," Major Tosca said to Vernya. "It's time to set the school on fire."

"I don't understand," she said, staring at him.

"Remember our fire insurance? We can make a small fortune."

"But I can't burn the school. *My* school!"

"Besides," Liz interrupted, "the flames could spread to the forest."

"That's exactly right. The trees are insured. Even if we can't log them, they're still worth something to us." Major Tosca looked at his wife. "Get the fuel from the storage shed, splash it around the school, then set it on fire."

Liz shook her head. "Major Tosca, you're crazy. You'll never collect the fire insurance."

"Of course I will."

"I doubt it. Haven't you noticed the pattern in your life? Every thing you do is a flop. The fancy restaurant was too big so it closed. Then the newspaper bombed, and the printing shop was a lemon, too. Now the life insurance scam has failed, and so will this fire insurance racket. Give it up, Major. *It won't work.*"

"You're wrong, Liz." He smiled. "It's true I've had a string of bad luck, but now things are finally going my way." He turned to Vernya. "Once the fire is burning well, take the small motorboat to Ukee. Then get the car and drive to the States. I'll meet you in Portland, at our favourite hotel."

"What about these kids?"

"Let me worry about them," he grinned. "I've got it all worked out, sweetheart."

Liz grabbed the woman's arm. "Don't do it, Vernya!"

"Please, Vernya!" Tom exclaimed.

But they were ignored. Without saying a word, Vernya left the wheelhouse. Major Tosca revved up the engine, and the launch slipped slowly out of the boathouse. Turning to the window, Tom saw the first light of dawn creeping into the eastern sky. Waves tossed on the grey ocean and slapped against the shoreline below the buildings of the deserted school. A minute later, Vernya came out of a shed dragging a metal container. As she crossed the wild grass in the direction of the nearest building, Tom felt sick.

"There's fuel in that container for the fire. The island doesn't have a chance."

Heading the launch into the waves, Major Tosca gave the engine full power. The deck vibrated, and they heard water smacking against the hull as the school was left behind. Soon they could see only the outline of the island's beautiful forest.

"There it goes!" Major Tosca cried shortly after. "What a sight!"

Looking up, Tom saw a glow in the sky above Nearby Island. It flared red and orange, then suddenly exploded into a hundred different colours. "The chem lab just blew up," he moaned. "It's all over now."

12

For an hour the launch headed south without anyone speaking.

Tom managed to doze for a while, then suddenly woke. He looked out the window at the stormy seas leaping around the launch. Foam blew off the waves and splattered against the glass in front of his eyes.

The two men stood by the wheel watching the storm. Major Tosca was pale, but Axe's face was empty of emotion.

"Axe," Tom said. "I have to know something."

The big man glanced his way. "What?"

"Why did you escape from the *Lady Rose* in the Zodiac?"

"I saw you people staring at me. You thought I killed Mrs. Tosca because I'd been fired."

"Where did you go?"

"To Nearby Island, to hide out. I know that island better than anyone but Mosquito Joe. I was watching the school from the forest when you kids came and got locked up. I tried to help you."

"I'm sorry. We didn't understand." As the big man shrugged, Tom looked at Major Tosca. The man's hands trembled as he stared at the waves leaping around the launch. "This is awful," he groaned. "Why is the weather always against me?"

At that moment the engine spluttered, roared back to life, then died.

Looking surprised, Major Tosca pressed the starter button. Nothing happened. Again he tried it, wiggling the key back and forth. "What's wrong with this thing?" He slammed his hand against the starter and turned to Axe. "Fix it!"

"I'm a printer. I can't fix boats."

"You've got to!" He pointed toward the shore. "You see that white water? There are rocks all along the coast. If this launch runs ashore, it'll be smashed to pieces." Desperately he turned to Tom and Liz. "Help me!"

Liz stood up, fighting to keep her balance as the launch wallowed helplessly in the big waves. Suddenly the coast was much closer. The waves were driving the launch remorselessly toward the rocks, where water leapt high into the air. Beyond the rocks, the trees of the forest bent low under the blasting wind.

"I've figured out the problem," Liz said moments later. "I'm surprised you couldn't, Major."

"*Fix it!*" the man screamed.

"I can't." Liz pointed at a gauge near the wheel. "You're out of fuel. Fighting this storm must have used up all the gas."

"You're lying." Major Tosca stared at the gauge and gripped the wheel. "We're going to die," he moaned. "Oh, no."

"Isn't there anything we can do? Maybe we can use that lifeboat on the roof."

Tom shook his head. "I doubt if that would help." He grabbed the table as the boat heeled over, then righted itself. "What about the radio? Maybe a Coast Guard boat is close by."

As Liz staggered across the cabin to the radio, the launch shook under the power of the sea. She flicked some switches, turned a dial and picked up the microphone. "*Mayday, Mayday.* My name is Liz Austen. I'm in the launch from Vernya Tosca's school. We are about one hour south of Nearby Island, drifting ashore without fuel. *Mayday, Mayday.* Do you read me?" As she put down the microphone, everyone stared at the radio. It whistled and squealed, but no words came out.

"It's hopeless!" Major Tosca said. "We're almost on the rocks!"

The power of the storm was overwhelming. Outside the wheelhouse the noise of the waves pounding against the shore was terrible, and Tom gripped the brass railing in horror as the launch was lifted high on a foaming wave and then slammed into a rock. Somehow it survived the blow and wallowed back into the sea.

Axe staggered toward them. His face was soaked with spray. "I'm going ashore with a rope. It's our only chance. I'll try to tie the rope to that big rock up there." He pointed to the top of the rocks. "When the rope's tight, you'll have to swing along it, hand-over-hand."

"Don't risk it," Tom shouted, but it was useless to argue. Axe moved forward to the bow and picked up the launch's mooring line. Climbing over the railing, he waited for the next wave to slam the launch against the rocks. Then he jumped.

"Axe!"

For a horrible moment Tom could see nothing. Then he wiped spray out of his eyes and saw Axe clinging to the rocks. Somehow he had managed to hold tight to the mooring rope, and now he dragged it behind as he crawled slowly up the rocks. He was lost from sight as the launch rolled in the waves, then righted itself and was again lifted into the air. With a bone-jarring crash it landed between two rocks.

"This is our chance," Tom yelled. "Axe has made it to the top."

High above the surging waves, Axe stood beside a large rock which jutted up alone. He wrapped the rope around it and then, suddenly, it stretched tightly between the rock and the launch.

"We'll drown!" Major Tosca screamed.

There was no time to argue with the man. Tom climbed over the rail and reached for the mooring line. Taking a deep breath, he jumped free of the launch. The rope dug into his fingers, and for a sickening moment his body swung wildly in the air above the rocks. Then he began to shift his hands along the taut line. The wind tore at his body, shrieking and howling, and the roar of the pounding sea was terrible, but within a minute he had moved far enough along the line to drop safely to the rocks. Crawling up the slippery slope, he waited for Liz to join him. Then they turned toward the launch.

The sea was beginning to destroy it. The mast had come down and lay broken across the wheelhouse. Several windows were smashed, and the hull had been split by the battering on the rocks. As they watched, a huge wave foamed in and lifted the launch free of the rocks where it had been wedged. As the boat rose into the air, the mooring line snapped.

Half the line whistled past Tom's head to smash into the rocks. The other half lashed like a whip toward the launch. It knocked down Major Tosca as the launch rolled back into the foaming water.

"He's not getting up! The line knocked him out."

The boat rolled to one side, but somehow the railing kept Major Tosca's body from falling into the sea. Then, with a splintering crash, the wheelhouse door was smashed open by the cartons containing the printing press, which fell into the sea.

Tom watched helplessly as the boat continued to rock back and forth in the raging sea. Suddenly he pointed at the wheelhouse.

"There's someone in there!"

The boat heeled over, then righted itself. As it did, a woman staggered out of the wheelhouse. Quickly she climbed to the roof and released the small lifeboat. Tom stared with unbelieving eyes.

"It's Nikki!"

She lowered the lifeboat to the deck of the launch and

then climbed down herself. Pulling the boat forward to the bow, Nikki dragged Major Tosca inside.

Tom, Liz and Axe scrambled down the rocks, then watched tensely as Nikki manoeuvred the lifeboat to an opening in the railing. Waiting until the launch rolled close to the waves, she pushed the lifeboat into the sea and then jumped inside. Grabbing a safety rope, she held on tightly as the lifeboat was lifted toward the rocks by the surging waves.

The instant it slammed against the rocks, Tom and Liz grabbed the safety ropes. As Axe lifted out Major Tosca, Nikki scrambled free of the lifeboat. Blood poured from a wound in the Major's head, and his lips were blue, but then he moaned and they knew he was still alive.

With Axe carrying Major Tosca, they climbed toward a cluster of rocks which gave shelter from the wind. Nikki wiped the blood away from the Major's wound, then tore her coat to make a rough bandage. Pressing this to the man's head, she looked at Tom and Liz.

"I'm so glad you're safe."

"Where were you, Nikki?"

"In the cabin. I couldn't get out because something was blocking the door."

"It was those cartons. Thank goodness they fell overboard. But how'd you get into the cabin?"

"When Andrew got back to Ukee in the cruiser, he phoned me. He said you'd missed the meeting at 2100 hours, but that you'd be okay on the beach until morning. I didn't agree, so I set off for Nearby Island in my boat. I went along the shore, calling you, and finally reached the school. I found the launch warming up, then saw you in the field with Warwick and Vernya."

"Did you see her gun?"

Nikki nodded. "I realized they'd be taking you in the launch. I slipped into the boathouse and hid in the cabin. But I couldn't do anything to help you because of the gun, and then the cartons were piled against the cabin door and I was trapped. When the storm hit I couldn't push the door open, and it was so noisy you couldn't hear me calling for help."

Liz held out her hand. "Nikki, I want to apologize."

"What for?"

"I really thought you'd killed Vernya on the *Lady Rose*. I feel so dumb."

Nikki smiled. "No hard feelings, Liz." Taking off her coat, she wrapped it around Major Tosca. Then she climbed to the top of the rocks. She shielded her eyes, studying the coast, before returning. "The storm's dying down, but it doesn't look good. There's still a lot of white water between those rocks and the shore. We'll have to wait it out."

Liz looked up at the sky. "Did you hear something?"

Scrambling from their shelter, Tom stared at the grey clouds above. A small plane was coming their way. Running to the top of the rocks, he screamed and waved his arms. The plane swooped low overhead, the pilot waved, then it rose in a circle and returned, wingtips waggling. "She's seen us! We're saved!"

Liz came to his side. "I wonder how they found us so fast?"

"Maybe they heard your Mayday message on the

radio." Tom looked at the launch, still being pounded against the rocks. "That wreck would be easy to spot from the air."

Within an hour, a helicopter was hovering above their rocky perch and Major Tosca was being winched toward its belly in a rescue sling. As Tom watched, Liz suddenly grabbed his arm and pointed out to sea. "Look!"

Coming out of the north was a sleek cruiser. White waves curled away from its bow as it rapidly approached, then cut its speed. Andrew appeared from the wheelhouse, holding a megaphone. He lifted it to his mouth, and his words came clearly across the water.

"Liz Austen! We've got a date today."

13

Two days later, Tom was again on the ocean.

This time the sun burned down from a clear sky. The bright beams sparkled off the water which was so calm that the idea of storms seemed impossible. In the distance, snowcapped mountains rose above Vancouver Island.

"This is paradise," Tom said, smiling at Bunni. They were sprawled on seats in the stern of a powerful motor-boat as it roared south from Tofino. With them were Nikki and her boyfriend, Dr. Darren Pickup. A professor at the University of British Columbia, Dr. Pickup was a world-famous expert on whales. He had promised Tom a real treat on this trip, but had refused to give details.

"You know," Tom said, looking at the man's brown

hair and moustache, "I can't believe he's a professor. He seems way too young."

"He sure is cute," Bunni replied. "That's all I know."

Tom laughed. "You sound like my sister." Lifting his camera, he took a picture of Dr. Pickup then smiled. "That'll show Liz what she missed today."

"Is she with Andrew?"

"Yup." Tom glanced at Bunni, looking wonderful with her blond hair tossing in the wind. Going forward, he whispered something to Nikki and gave her the camera. Returning to Bunni's side, he beamed at the camera while the shutter clicked. "This picture's for Dietmar," he said, grinning.

"Who?"

"Oh, just a guy I know. He'll want to see how I spent my summer."

Bunni sighed. "School soon. I can't believe it."

"Maybe I'll write you from Winnipeg."

"That would be great."

Tom smiled at her, then looked at Nikki. "Thanks for a fantastic summer!"

"Come again next year," she said, moving back to the stern. "I'm only sorry about the trouble with Warwick. All that nasty business probably spoiled your holiday."

"No way," Tom grinned. "My life is detective work."

Bunni looked at her sister. "What will happen to the Major?"

"He's facing a long time behind bars." Nikki shook her head. "Poor Warwick. He's so charming, but such a loser."

"You know," Tom said, "I should have realized there

might be an insurance fraud involved. I remember how you thought the Toscas had torched their first house for the fire insurance money."

"Sure, but what about the life insurance? You couldn't have suspected anything."

"Well, I do remember that Bunni and I talked about blanks and capsules of fake blood, on our trip to Long Beach. That should have helped me figure it out."

"It was a tricky scam," Nikki said. "Do you know who I suspected of shooting Vernya?"

Tom shook his head.

"Mac."

"How come?"

"Because Vernya had fired him long ago, after promising him a home on the island."

"He had even more reason to hate the Toscas," Tom pointed out. "That was rotten of them to steal his dog."

Stopping the motorboat just off a small bay, Dr. Pickup moved to the stern with some binoculars. "If you watch carefully through these, Tom, you may see your first whale."

With excited eyes, Tom scanned the shimmering waters of the bay. "Is that it?" he asked, staring at a back flipper that rose into the air above the water.

"Sure thing." Dr. Pickup smiled. "That little grey whale has been in the bay all summer, feeding. As you see, she lies on her side with the flipper breaking the surface while she eats."

Bunni looked through the binoculars. "That's neat! What's she eating?"

"Mud shrimp and tube worms. She takes sand and everything else from the bottom into her mouth, then turns onto her side while separating the food. After that she spits out the sand and mud. They look like smoke coming out of her mouth."

"Can we get closer?" Tom asked.

Dr. Pickup shook his head. "Our boat might frighten her."

Tom studied the flipper, wishing it was possible to see more of the whale. "Thanks for bringing us here," he said as Dr. Pickup started the boat. "Is there any chance of seeing any more whales?"

"We may spot some on the way home. The boats that take tourists whale-watching from Tofino and Ucluelet often see grey whales this time of year." He smiled at Tom. "I've actually petted a grey whale."

"You're kidding!"

"They're very gentle, really, and this one seemed curious. It circled our boat, then suddenly its head appeared beside us, like a pet wanting its ears scratched."

"But grey whales are huge," Bunni said. "Couldn't it have sunk you?"

"There's always a risk that they'll accidentally lift a small boat out of the water. After all, they're still wild animals."

For a long time they headed south without anyone speaking. Then Dr. Pickup suddenly pointed toward shore. "Quick, look at that!" Rising out of the water was a large black head with a white chin. Sunlight reflected from the creature's glistening body as it rose higher, revealing white flashes behind its eyes. Its head and upper body hovered above the blue water for a moment, then gradually sank beneath the surface.

"I don't believe it!" Tom exclaimed. "That was a

killer whale."

Dr. Pickup grinned. "Wasn't that a splendid sight? The whale was spy-hopping."

"What does that mean?"

"Sometimes killer whales rise up from the water like that to spy around. That one must have heard our boat and wanted to take a look." He pointed at Tom's camera. "Did you get it on film?"

"I forgot! I was too excited."

"We may see another. They travel in pods, which is a group like a family, so there'll be others around. Killer whales mostly live on the other side of Vancouver Island, but we know of two pods that also come out here."

"Look at that!" Bunni shouted.

Close by, a killer whale had suddenly leapt clear of the sea. Its magnificent black body shone in the sun above the waves. Then it spiralled over to land on its back. As white water shot everywhere, it disappeared from sight.

"I got a picture!" Tom yelled. "At least I remembered this time."

"That's called breaching," Dr. Pickup said. "The whales build up a tremendous speed underwater, as much as forty-eight kilometres an hour, then burst from the surface. Our research suggests that breaching is just a form of play, but it may have other purposes. There's still a lot to learn."

Bunni looked carefully at him. "I didn't know your work was so interesting. That killer whale was the most exciting thing I've ever seen."

Nikki smiled at her sister. "Now you understand

why Greenpeace has worked so hard to stop whaling. People have no right to hunt these creatures. They should be left in peace."

"But people don't hunt killer whales."

"Sure they do, to put them on display as tourist attractions. A place in San Diego called Sea World planned to capture one hundred killer whales off the Alaskan coast. Can you believe it? *One hundred* of them! It's not fair to keep these animals in captivity. Thank goodness the Sierra Club went to court and stopped the hunt. But we'll always have to be on guard for the whales, and our rainforests, and endangered birds like the bald eagle, and lots of other wildlife. Even the grizzly bears in the Rocky Mountains are threatened by humans!"

Bunni smiled at her. "Take it easy. You're getting steamed up again."

"You're right." Nikki hugged her. "It's just that I want you and Tom, and every kid in the world, to care about these things."

"I'm beginning to understand. I admit I didn't care about them logging Nearby Island, but I wouldn't want those whales to be hurt."

Dr. Pickup turned from the wheel to look at her. "But logging can hurt the whales, too, Bunni. The greys, like that little one we saw, feed in quiet waters. After clear-cut logging, siltation patterns are ruined. The result can be the destruction of kelp beds where whales feed."

"But what can people do?"

"Write the government about your feelings, and support groups like Greenpeace and the Sierra Club that are fighting for our environment. It costs a lot of money to battle an organization like Sea World in court, but that's our best hope. If we stick together, maybe we can even stop nuclear war."

"The thought of war really scares me."

"It used to frighten me, too, Bunni, but I feel better as time goes by. There hasn't been a major world war since 1945. The atomic bomb was used to end it, and people were horrified by the destruction. Nobody wants to repeat that mistake. The leaders of the superpowers are ordinary people like you and me. They have children and grandchildren, and they care about our world too. So they've avoided using their nuclear weapons, and meanwhile the peace movement continues to grow." He smiled. "Things will be fine, as long as you kids grow up willing to help protect our planet."

Nikki reached to squeeze his hand. "That's quite a message, Darren."

He laughed. "I guess I get steamed up, too. Anyway, we're almost at Nearby Island. Then we can enjoy our picnic."

Tom looked across the sea at the wispy clouds drifting around the summit of the island. "Thank goodness Vernya didn't set that fire."

"But what did happen?" Bunni asked. "Wasn't there a fire at the school?"

Tom nodded. "Apparently Vernya dragged all the chemicals from the chem lab into the open field and piled wood over them. She set the wood on fire and ran. When the chemicals exploded, it made a huge bonfire. That was the glow we saw in the sky. Later the storm hit, and rain doused the fire, but it would have burned out on its own, anyway."

"But why did Vernya bother doing all that?"

"I guess she wanted to fool her husband. If he hadn't seen flames, he might have gone back to set a fire himself." Tom sighed. "Poor Vernya, in love with a jerk like that."

Nikki looked at him. "Some day, Tom, you'll find out love isn't always easy to understand."

He gazed at Nikki, not knowing what she meant. Then he looked across the sea at the shimmering beauty of Nearby Island. "I don't think Vernya ever really wanted her island to be destroyed. She was taken in by the Major and his phoney promises to replant trees. I'm sure he never intended to do that, because it takes money and commitment—two things he didn't have a lot of."

"Do you think Vernya will get a long prison term?" Bunni asked.

"It's hard to say. At least she turned herself in to the police. That may help her."

"What about Axe?"

"I'm afraid he's in trouble about those counterfeit lottery tickets."

"And Mosquito Joe? Is he alive, or dead?"

Nikki smiled. "Don't worry about that hermit, Tom. He's a survivor. When the loggers started work, he abandoned his shack and hid in the forest. Now the logging's been stopped for sure, so he'll be able to live in peace on the island."

"I'm glad he's safe."

Dr. Pickup smiled at Tom. "You demonstrators showed a lot of spirit. That helped save the rainforest."

As they entered the quiet beauty of Captain Cook Cove, Tom sighed happily. "Anyway, I'm sure glad the island has survived."

Nikki nodded. "Too bad you're going back to Winnipeg. We could use your help on the Queen Charlotte Islands."

"What do you mean?"

"I'm flying up there tomorrow. It's my turn to be buried in front of the bulldozers."

"But why?"

"A company plans to start logging old-growth forest on one of those islands next week. After that, there are fifteen more places on this coast where the rainforest is threatened."

"You mean the fight isn't over?" he asked in dismay.

Nikki shook her head. "We're going to need help for a very long time."

"Then you can count on me," Tom said. "It's my world, too."

About the Author

SANDI KRASOWSKI, *THE CHRONICLE-JOURNAL*, THUNDER BAY

After working as a journalist, Eric Wilson became a teacher in White Rock, British Columbia. His Grade 8 students hated books, so Eric wrote them an adventure novel called *Fat Boy Speeding*. Those kids' enthusiasm for the story led Eric into his career as an author. But he's still often in schools, meeting his readers.

Researching this mystery, Eric travelled on the *Lady Rose* and explored the rainforest after dark. Since this book was first published, the government of B.C. has made many changes to protect the province's rainforests.

MURDER ON *THE CANADIAN*
A Tom Austen Mystery

ERIC WILSON

The porter stood in the doorway of the sleeping car, waving his arm. "Come on, man!" he yelled. "Move those feet!"

The agonizing sound of a woman's scream hurls Tom Austen into the middle of a murder plot on board the sleek passenger train *The Canadian*. Who is responsible for the death of lovely Catherine Saks? As Tom investigates the strange collection of travelers who share Car 165, he gets closer and closer to the truth ... and then, without warning, he is suddenly face-to-face with the killer, and his own life is threatened in the most alarming way possible.

"In Murder on The Canadian, *there is excitement from the start; the first dozen pages produce a bomb, a 'deadly enemy." ... there are plenty of suspects to lay false trails, and the action moves as fast as the train."*
                                    – Times Literary Supplement

ISBN 1-55143-151-3, $4.99
Accelerated Reader Quiz #21931

VANCOUVER NIGHTMARE
A Tom Austen Mystery

ERIC WILSON

Tom tried to go lower but his foot slipped and dropped into open air. An electric shock of fear passed through him ...

A chance meeting with a drug dealer named Spider takes Tom Austen into the grim streets of Vancouver's Skid Road, where he poses as a runaway while searching for information to help the police smash a gang that is hooking young kids on drugs.

Suddenly unmasked as a police agent, Tom is trapped in Vancouver's nightmarish underworld as the gang closes in, determined to get rid of the young meddler at any cost.

"'The coffin was open, the air black and musty all around.' Who could resist a mystery begun in such a fashion? This fast-paced tale of drug smuggling and deceit will be an instant success ..."
— Canadian Book Review Annual

ISBN 1-55143-149-1, $4.99
Accelerated Reader Quiz #41288

DISNEYLAND HOSTAGE
A Liz Austen Mystery

ERIC WILSON

The air was blasted by the huge rotors of a helicopter which roared in above the wall and hovered over the fort, shaking us with the force of the wind storm it created.

On her own during a California holiday, Liz Austen is plunged into the middle of an international plot when a boy named Ramón disappears from his room at the Disneyland Hotel. Has Ramón been taken hostage? Before Liz can answer that question, her own safety is threatened when terrorists strike at the most unlikely possible target: Disneyland itself.

"… will leave young readers looking eagerly forward to more Liz Austen adventures."
– Midwest Book Review

"The breakneck action, interesting settings, and contemporary issues will draw avid or reluctant mystery readers alike."
– School Library Journal

ISBN 1-55143-174-2, $4.99
Accelerated Reader Quiz #35396

THE CASE OF THE GOLDEN BOY
A Tom Austen Mystery

ERIC WILSON

Headlights shone in the distance; a police car, moving fast. It swerved to a stop by the curb, then Officer Larson leapt out and ran swiftly inside. What was going on?

An investigation into the kidnapping of his schoolmate leads young Tom Austen to the seedy Golden Boy Cafe and an unexpected encounter with a desperate criminal. After getting one step too close to the kidnappers, Tom is taken prisoner and needs all his wits to survive.

". . . the heroes exhibit integrity and character that readers can admire."

– Today's Librarian

ISBN 1-55143-173-4, $4.99

THE KOOTENAY KIDNAPPER
A Tom Austen Mystery

ERIC WILSON

Silence came to the cave, broken only by the drip of water on rock. Cold and loneliness spread through Tom's tired body.

Suddenly Tattoo's hand lashed out.

What is the secret lurking in the ruins of a lonely ghost town in the mountains of British Columbia? Solving this mystery is only one of the challenges facing Tom Austen after he arrives in B.C. with this sidekick, Dietmar Oban, and learns that a young girl has disappeared without a trace. Then a boy is kidnapped, and electrifying events quickly carry Tom to a breathtaking climax deep underground in Cody Caves, where it is forever night ...

"*Set in the mountainous interior of British Columbia,* The Kootenay Kidnapper *is about streetproofing ... Wilson weaves an important, current theme into a believable mystery.*"

– The Ottawa Citizen

1-55143-171-8, $4.99 pb

CODE RED AT THE SUPERMALL
A Tom and Liz Austen Mystery

ERIC WILSON

They swam past gently moving strands of seaweed and pieces of jagged coral, then Tom almost choked in horror. A shark was coming right at him, ready to strike.

Have you ever visited a shopping mall that has sharks and piranhas, a triple-loop rollercoaster, 22 waterslides, an Ice Palace, submarines, 828 stores, and a major mystery to solve?

Soon after Tom and Liz Austen arrive at West Edmonton Mall, a bomber strikes and they must follow a trail that leads through the fabled splendors of the supermall … to hidden danger.

". . . the heroes exhibit integrity and character that readers can admire."

– Today's Librarian

ISBN 1-55143-172-6, $4.99
Accelerated Reader Quiz #35395

VAMPIRES OF OTTAWA
A Liz Austen Mystery

ERIC WILSON

Suddenly the vampire rose up from behind a tombstone and fled, looking like an enormous bat with his cape streaming behind him in the moonlight.

Within the walls of a gloomy estate known as Blackwater, Liz Austen discovers the strange world of Baron Nicolai Zaba, a man who lives in constant fear. What is the secret of the ancient chapel's underground vault? Why are the words "In Evil Memory" scrawled on a wall? Who secretly threatens the Baron? All the answers lie within these pages but be warned: *reading this book will make your blood run cold.*

"From the very beginning, excitement fills this fast-moving mystery. Readers who like the Nancy Drew and Hardy Boys mysteries will find the adventures of Tom and Liz Austen equally exciting."

– Library Talk

ISBN 1-55143-228-5, $4.99

Collect all of these thrilling Eric Wilson Mysteries!